RETURN TO MAPLEWOOD

ELIZABETH BROMKE

RETURN TO MAPLEWOOD

Cover design by German Creative
Cover photography by Donya Nedomam,
photoweges, misfire, and tycoon
First Edition- January 2019
Published by:
Elizabeth Bromke

For my mom, who made me the woman I am today.

When the Lord closes a door, somewhere he opens
a window.
- *The Sound of Music*

CHAPTER ONE

Three quick raps cut through the shards of hot water beating down on Anna's lithe body.

"Anna? Hurry up! Our reservation is for six o'clock, and I still need to dry my hair," Jenna called from the other side of the hotel bathroom door.

Anna Delaney twisted the silver faucet handle, opened the shower door, and reached for her towel. She dabbed the droplets from her skin and assessed herself in the mirror. She'd lost five pounds since New Year's, and it showed. Her collarbones popped out from under her sharp jawline, and her waistline dipped where it should. Anna couldn't tell if she liked being officially thin, but it wasn't as if she was trying.

The last few months had been hard on her as she watched her sister fall madly in love with Kurt Cutler, who just so happened to be Anna's handsome, smart, kind-hearted boss. She hadn't intended on setting them up, but that's exactly what happened when Anna arranged for her company to have their winter retreat at Mary's Maplewood Lodge.

Mary and Kurt were smitten with each other, and it was irritating. It wasn't that Anna was ever in love with Kurt, but for some reason she had clung to a bit of envy as she watched him head to Maplewood every other weekend, leaving her to handle weekend website traffic for their tech startup, FantasyCoin.

"Give me ten minutes!" Anna called back through the door. She pulled her shower cap off, allowing for her reddish waves to bloom around her. Her hair fell well below chest level and in every which way. Anna and her brother, Alan, were the only redheads of the six Delaney children, but she particularly rocked the strawberry locks. Paired with her green eyes, creamy skin, and tall stature, men and women alike would often do a double take when they saw her.

She stowed her shower cap into the corner of the vanity and then tucked the towel around her body before starting in on her makeup routine.

Anna had left the fateful winter retreat early in order to address a server issue at the office. She didn't have to, but she definitely *wanted* to. The retreat hadn't been as enjoyable an experience largely because Kurt and Mary flirted nonstop in front of Anna and the rest of the company team. Once Anna had arrived home and called Mary to follow up, Mary accused her of misbehaving and acting jealous. Needless to say, Anna's bad attitude about it all had quadrupled, leaving her to turn to her girlfriends back home in Phoenix.

Once her friends heard from Anna and listened on as she described the most awkward third-wheel experience of her life, they thoughtfully booked a girls' trip to Vegas for a long weekend in late February. Something for Anna to look forward to, they assured her.

Deep down, Anna knew that the trip was less a consolation prize and more an excuse to party. It had become the norm in their little friend circle.

Anna had met Amber and Jenna in college at Southwestern Arizona. Jessica was Amber's cousin. The four of them made a formidable team. They spent the last decade encouraging each other to make bad decisions in the name of fun and freedom.

Anna didn't need therapy to know that they were toxic for each other.

But life was good with the girls around. Weekends were exciting, and they were almost always there for each other. It was exciting to have friends who weren't sisters. No one to judge or report back to Mom and Dad.

Anna finished her fifth coat of mascara and tossed the tube back onto the counter. Finally, she swung the door open to Jenna, who was too glued to her phone to look up.

"Be out in fifteen," Jenna mumbled as she crossed into the bathroom, scrolling away.

Anna strode through into their shared bedroom. Amber and Jessica were in the connected suite, and Anna could hear them watching trash TV through the open door.

In late December, the foursome had booked the two suites in a timeshare that Jenna's parents owned. They were on the end of the strip, so they'd have to grab a Lyft to make it to the new restaurant where they were starting their evening.

Anna was in awe of Jenna's family. They weren't filthy rich, but they did well for themselves. They vacationed a few times a year, and Jenna didn't even have to pay for her own car insurance or cell phone. Jenna's upbringing was a far cry from Anna's early years on the farm, where she got up at the crack of dawn every day and milked cows and collected eggs as if she lived in the 1800s.

Anna knew she would never really go back to Maplewood. The high life was where she made her home now.

CHAPTER TWO

Dutch McCree booted up the computer in his Scottsdale home office. He had never expected to find himself in one of the more expensive neighborhoods of Phoenix, especially since he grew up in tiny little Bisbee, Arizona- where the only people with any real money were eclectic artists who eschewed the finer things anyway.

But, he wasn't complaining. Once Dutch struck gold with his construction company and nailed a contract to build a sprawling McMansion community north of Phoenix, he told his family to pack up. Dutch, his parents, his wife, and their daughter CaitlinJo were moving to the big city, and he was able to foot the bill.

It was a big adjustment for his small-town family. His dad had worked in the copper mines until they shut down, and his mom tended bar on Brewery Gulch until Dutch and Megan invited them to move in and help take care of Caitlin.

Dutch figured that the big move would be an opportunity to establish separate living spaces again, and so he bought his parents a two-bedroom on Hole 9, two streets over from Dutch and Megan, who spread themselves out in a spacious four-bedroom closer to the Country Club.

The two McCree families lived in relative luxury, and Dutch's business had yet to flag. He made smart investments, but other than the posh living quarters, Dutch and Megan were smart with spending. Megan gave up waitressing and became a stay-at-home mom, watching soap operas and playing with CaitlinJo. It was bliss.

Until the car accident.

It was a Saturday evening in November, two years earlier. Megan went out with friends. Dutch stayed at home with

CaitlinJo. An elderly woman who had no business being behind the wheel plowed into the driver's side door.

Megan died instantaneously.

Even two years later, Dutch had no intentions of seeking out a new girlfriend or stepmom for Caitlin. Losing Megan devastated the family. CaitlinJo had been a toddler at the time, but she seemed to absorb the shock and trauma as much or more than Dutch.

Dutch considered consolidating houses with his parents once again, but they refused, knowing full-well that one day Dutch and CaitlinJo would be able to move on. Dutch, of course, disagreed.

Now, he leaned forward in his wooden office chair and clicked around until his work email populated. Forty-seven new messages.

Dutch let out a sigh. He missed having Megan around to help with the administrative duties. He hated computers and phones and anything with a battery, really. He glanced up at the clock, noting that he'd have to drive Cait over to her Wednesday preschool class in less than an hour.

Chugging away, he made it through about half the messages before his precious little dark-haired four-year-old yawned her way into his office.

"Daddy, whatcha workin' on?" She asked as she crawled into Dutch's lap.

"Emails, baby. How'd you sleep?"

"Not good, but I can't remember," she replied, rubbing the sleep from her eyes. Dutch chuckled and buried his face in her hair, planting a kiss on the back of her head before rising, CaitlinJo in his arms.

"Well, maybe a big pancake breakfast will help wake you up?"

She squealed in response and wriggled down from his arms, dancing her way to the kitchen table, where she waited for

Dutch to bring out the pancake mix, a bowl, and a glass of water. Dutch and CaitlinJo had become accustomed to doing things the convenient way. As such, he poured an approximation of water into the bowl and followed with the instant mix.

"Here's a spoon, now stir slowly, Cait. Rushed pancakes taste no good," he reminded her as he lit a gas burner and set a skillet squarely on top of it.

Together, the pair cooked up the pancakes, doused them in syrup, gobbled them down, and laughed all the while. Dutch had to remind himself that even when he was feeling his lowest, he had CaitlinJo. She was the light of his life.

He let his sweet baby girl pick out her outfit and dress herself as he waited again in his office, clicking through another page of emails. Just as he heard CaitlinJo slam her door and trot down the stairs, his eyes skimmed over a recent email from one of his two secretaries, Jeanette.

Dutch,

Maplewood Project going fine, but I'll need you to come to town in the next couple weeks to take a look at an expansion proposal. Michael is hoping to add another 20 units and wants your oversight. Let me know when you can get away.

—Jeanette

"Daddy, time to go or we'll be late!" Cait was pulling on his chair back.

Great, he thought to himself. *Never should have taken on an out-of-town project.*

"Just a minute, baby," he waved her away absently as he pecked out a quick response.

Jeanette,

Thanks for update. Michael isn't the project manager- I am. I'll get back to you on my travel plans.

—D.M.

Michael Erinhard was the best architect east of Phoenix, and he was worth every penny. He was a ticket to success for the new luxury homes community that Dutch had been hired to build in little Maplewood.

Dutch had never been to Maplewood and had only visited any mountain range maybe once or twice in his life. He had a lot to learn about construction in a different climate and at a different altitude, and Michael had been invaluable to him. They worked very closely to make sure that the homes would be up to code and survive rain and snow, especially since they were building at the end of winter, a less-than-ideal construction season.

Still, Michael seemed to be growing a little over-confident that the community would bring in so many buyers. Maplewood was not the premier tourist destination for Phoenicians or Tucsonans. The White Mountains were.

He resolved to ask his local secretary, Jody, to take a look at his calendar and find a date or two. Why hadn't he just had Jody run admin on this project, anyway? Too many people to please. Too many cooks in the kitchen. But, he needed both women *and* Michael to make everything run smoothly.

Dutch was simply forced to give up some of his control.

CHAPTER THREE

The girls had just finished dinner and paid their separate tabs as Jenna stood, tugging down on her mini dress to avoid flashing the other diners.

"Where to now, ladies?" She demanded, hands pressed onto her hips, the bar lights framing her from behind.

Amber groaned, "I am stuffed and tired. How about a night in for once?"

Jenna pointedly stared at Amber's bloated gut. "For one, we are literally in Las Vegas. We are not calling it a night. And secondly, maybe getting up and dancing will make you, er, feel better," she let her eyes scan the rest of Amber's stocky body.

Jenna regularly advocated for fasting, extreme diets, and two-a-day workouts. Jessica and Amber were often her audience, especially Amber- who enjoyed over-indulging and binge-drinking.

Anna looked to Jessica, to see if Amber's own cousin would come to her defense. When she noted that Jessica was too busy scrolling through Facebook, Anna cleared her throat.

"Let's just get drinks in the hotel bar."

"Um, no. We aren't lame. Don't turn me into a forty-something with a bedtime, Anna. What's gotten into you, anyway? You're usually the wildest of us all," Jenna snarled back, suspicion filling her voice.

"Compromise time, ladies. Let's just do ReveRb like we had talked about. We can stay an hour or whatever. That way Jenna gets to dance."

"Fine. Vamos," Jenna directed, her clutch gripped tightly in her manicured, bone-thin fingers as she stalked toward the door. She knew the others would follow. And they did.

After five minutes of waiting for another Lyft and another five minutes cruising two hotel lengths down the strip, the group arrived at ReveRb, a relatively exclusive club that had opened months earlier. Anna knew this because she and her friends had attended the opening. It occurred to her that she probably went to Vegas too often, but no one could argue Vegas wasn't a great way to burn off steam and chill. She loved to dance and she loved clubbing.

As the girls strode smoothly to the velvet rope that framed the concrete walkway, they passed a group of three men. The guys looked younger, but were undoubtedly hot and undoubtedly on the prowl.

Anna ignored them and cut left along the rope and up to the line that bled out from the gaping door. She wrapped her blazer more snugly around her. Since dinner, the temp had dropped a bit. That plus an evening breeze gave her a chill.

Anna used her other hand to pull her long, red hair around her neck and over her shoulder, tucking it like a scarf. She nibbled at her lip and craned her neck around the unmoving line.

A shriek of laughter cut through her irritation at standing outside in the cold night. She whipped her head back around to see that Jessica and Jenna had been caught by the group of guys and were laughing wildly.

Amber had pulled up behind Anna. As she turned back around to Anna, she rolled her eyes and sighed. "Do you want to drag them over or should I?" she joked.

But Anna was not in the mood for a joke. At one point in this trip, she had lost her appetite for Vegas. She couldn't put her finger on it. Maybe it was Jenna's ongoing rudeness. Maybe Anna didn't want to go to work on Monday feeling gross. Whatever it was, she took matters into her own hands.

"I'll be back." She brushed by Amber and stomped up to the newly-formed group of five. "Don't want to lose our place in line, do we ladies?" Anna growled through gritted teeth and hooked her fingers on Jessica's purse. The girls' laughter had puttered out, and Anna couldn't tell if the men were glaring at her or sizing her up.

"You do not wanna go to ReveRb, trust us," the tallest one replied. Anna couldn't help but notice he was her type. Young. Boyishly handsome. Total frat boy material. But the edge to his voice turned her off.

"Why? We went last fall. It was great." Anna kept her voice even as she crossed her lithe arms and glanced back toward poor Amber who was watching nervously.

"Because you've been invited to a private party," the tan one replied, his eyes on Jessica.

Jessica loved it, ogling him back. Jenna giggled. Anna rarely heard Jenna *giggle*. Cackle maybe, but not giggle.

The men were clearly attractive, and Anna felt another chill course through her. It wasn't the weather this time.

On trips past, Anna would have read the situation differently and probably let Amber wilt in line as she joined in flirting with handsome strangers.

But this whole weekend just felt… different.

"Sounds sketch," Anna shifted her weight into Jessica, trying to casually nudge her friend back to reality.

"Sounds cool to me," Jenna interrupted, avoiding eye contact with Anna. "Jess and I are game. Anna, aren't you?" Her voice rose slightly, but she kept her gaze trained on the tall one.

"Not tonight. Let's just hit the club and do our thing, come on Jen," Anna started to hear a pleading creep into her voice, and she felt a twinge of embarrassment.

Jenna finally whipped her head in Anna's direction.

"*Who* are you?" She snapped. "Just come with us. We can send Amber back to the room. She'll appreciate it." Jenna didn't bother to look in Amber's direction, but Jessica did and a shadow of pity crossed her delicate bone structure.

"Can I talk to you privately, Jen?" Anna lowered her voice, trying to break Jenna's trance. It worked, and Jenna flashed a smile and a wink at the boys before turning her back on them and leaning her head toward Anna, who dropped her voice further.

"I'm not feeling it. The hook-up thing, whatever. There are three of these guys and two of you. It's weird, Jen. Come on, let's bail." Anna looked down at her friend, her eyebrows pinched in worry.

Jenna didn't hesitate. "*You're* weird. What happened to 'needing to get it out of your system?' You were all talk when we planned this trip, and you've been dying to get away from the office. And your geeky boss. What's the deal, Anna?" Jenna glanced back as Jessica simply stared at the strangers.

"It's not what I thought it was going to be. Things have changed. I'll go to the club, but I don't want any part of this," Anna discreetly nodded back toward the panting boys.

"Suit yourself," Jenna spat as she pirouetted on her heel and away from Anna. "Alright boys, where are we going?"

CHAPTER FOUR

After dropping CaitlinJo at preschool, Dutch shot over to his current local project, a boutique shopping plaza up the road from the Country Club. Jody was scheduled to be there, rather than at the office, so that she could take notes for Dutch on any issues in the final phases.

"Hey, boss," Jody yawned over her shoulder at him as he walked through the unfinished doorway at the curb of the eatery.

Dutch was responsible for overseeing completion and quality of a vegan eatery, a custom hatter, a local coffee shop, and an organic vitamin joint.

After they hammered the last nail and peeled the caution tape off the front, Dutch knew he would never be back to that particular plaza. Sure, he made a point of becoming a patron of businesses that he built, but he couldn't get behind the vegan lifestyle or even the organic movement. As for coffee, he preferred Folgers. He didn't mind the custom hatter, but it did seem a little hifalutin' for his tastes, which were limited to worn baseball caps.

"Hi Jody, how's it going here? When are the front doors going in? That needs to have happened by now," Dutch crossed his arms and glanced around the almost-finished space.

"The boys just went to the back to rework something for the doors. They are going up shortly," Jody replied as she jotted a note to herself. "Want to do your walk-through?"

As Dutch and Jody carefully inspected each business space, he made note of various little things. Sawdust here, left-behind screws there, over-sprayed paint on a handrail, smudged glass, a loose bathroom faucet. His attention to detail was bar none, which was why he hired two secretaries to begin with. Having four ongoing projects throughout the valley and now Maplewood, he couldn't afford to get sloppy.

When they had finished the walk-through, his head carpenter and some underlings walked in a massive wooden door. Dutch quickly grabbed the front and pitched in, supporting the heavy beast as the others went about drilling and screwing and assessing.

When they had finished, Dutch asked Jody for the list of incidentals. He personally went through each item with the workmen, walking them into and out of every nook and cranny.

Once they took the list and got back to work, Dutch returned his attention to Jody again.

The husband in him had made a conscious decision to hire secretaries who were older and married. He didn't want to entangle himself in the same trouble he knew so many businessmen fell into. In addition to being cliché, affairs with subordinates were low budget.

Then again, it wasn't as if Dutch was even capable of being seduced. After Megan had died, his heart sealed. He had no more room for new love. It wouldn't happen.

"Jody, that new secretary I have up in Maplewood," Dutch started, scratching under his ball cap.

"Jeanette? Is everything okay with her?" Jody was quick to jump to conclusions.

"Oh yes, she's great," Dutch replied before catching Jody's face fall. "I mean she is good enough. What I was going to ask you is to find a weekend in my schedule to head up to Maplewood. Michael Erinhard wants to expand the project, but I have to take a look in person and work it out with him."

"Yessir." Jody dutifully put her pen to paper and whirled it around before stowing her little notebook back into her tote. "If that'll be it, Mr. McCree, I need to run to the bank and make a couple deposits now?"

"Yep, have a great day, Jody." They turned away from each other to go in their separate directions before Dutch remembered something. "Oh, and Jody? Was it you I had put together that ad in the Mountain News up there?"

"I don't know what you're talking about sir. Maybe you asked Jeanette? But I'm happy to take over on that and get it up and running?"

Dutch grinned. Jody and Jeanette had little in common. But, they were both eager to please him.

CHAPTER FIVE

Amber and Anna began to drag themselves back to the hotel on foot. Fresh air, Anna insisted. She was feeling too anxious to grab a car. She wanted to burn her nervous energy even if she was wearing heels. Amber always went along with everything, and so she didn't put up a fuss.

"I can't believe your cousin," Anna complained. "I mean, that behavior is typical of Jenna, but Jessica is way cooler than hooking up with strangers," Anna trailed off as she felt Amber screech to a halt behind her. "What?" She turned back, shifting her weight onto one hip.

"Are you kidding me?" Amber demanded.

Anna felt herself flush. She knew exactly what was coming next.

"Anna, you literally hook up with a new guy every weekend. And every guy you hook up with is a stranger." Amber uncrossed her arms and stomped ahead in her embarrassingly sensible flats.

"But," Anna started as she took off after her. "This is different."

Amber kept walking, not bothering to look behind but raising her voice. "How? Are you jealous that those guys didn't prey on you first? Is that how?"

Now it was Anna's turn to slow down. But Amber kept walking, her dark hair whipping behind her in the brisk breeze.

She instantly felt sick to her stomach, as though she had eaten something bad. She looked for a bench or a place to rest, fuming over the fact that Amber kept going, leaving Anna behind in the middle of Las Vegas Boulevard. She spotted a concrete flowerbed and stalked over to it. Once there, she plopped down onto the cool surface and pulled her phone out.

She saw that it was nearly ten o'clock, but she didn't care. Fondling her little necklace, she scrolled to Mary's name. The one sister she could trust to give her solid advice.

Six rings and a voicemail greeting later, Anna stabbed at the red End button and swiped back to her contacts.

Erica lived in Pennsylvania. And had kids. And was pregnant. Anna wasn't *that* desperate.

She settled on Roberta.

Please answer, Anna whispered as she pressed Send.

"Hey," came Roberta's throaty voice through the din of a no-doubt seedy establishment.

"Bo," Anna sat up straight. Roberta had gone by "Bo" since she was little, and it stuck. "Where are you?" Her eyebrows furrowed, and she hoped Bo wasn't on a date.

"The Cactus Moon. Where are *you*?" Bo sneered back.

She should have guessed. Since Bo had moved to Tucson in order to take a writing gig, she had spent Wednesday through Saturday nights at whatever honkytonk was offering the best drink special.

"Can you talk? I'm in Vegas. I need help," Anna's voice crumpled as she began to cry. She heard shuffling on the other end of the line before Bo came back on.

"Anna, what's going on? Are you safe? What are you doing in Vegas?"

Anna choked out her answers through sobs as she shielded her face from passersby. A Las Vegas Boulevard flowerbed didn't feel like a safe place to have an emotional breakdown.

"My... friends... all... ditched... me." She could taste her makeup washing into her mouth as she coughed on the last syllable.

Bo waited a beat before responding. "Breathe, Sis. Just breathe. Ditched you where? Are you in a safe place?"

Anna straightened up and wiped the wetness from her cheeks as she peered around her. She did not feel safe. She felt like her heart could break at any moment in a very public arena.

"Yes," she shuttered into the phone.

"Did you call Mary? Isn't she, like, the best choice for advice here?" Bo chuckled.

"She didn't answer."

Another moment passed before Bo sighed into the receiver. "Anna, what happened? Are you in your hotel room? What's going on, give me the story."

Anna wobbled up into a standing position and ran her hand down her pink sequined dress. She felt like a leftover Valentine. A trampy one.

But, she pulled herself together and teetered down the sidewalk between moving bachelorette parties and drunken lovebirds and, in hiccoughing spurts she spilled her story to her oldest sister.

Bo listened as Anna bemoaned the fact that she had no room to judge Jessica or Jenna for ditching her in favor of hot guys. She complained that Amber was right to be irritated with her. Finally, she admitted that she didn't know what she was doing with her life. She was a self-proclaimed man-using man-hater, but she was over it. In fact, she never wanted to go out with another man ever again.

"Real mature, Anna. Swearing off men is what got you into this crisis. I mean, I'm not one to talk here, but anyone can see that your anger is what got you here."

Anna was livid. "You *are* a freakin' hypocrite, Bo. When was the last time you were even at a family event? A year ago? Two?"

"Yeah, I am fully aware, Ann. But, it seems like you're hitting rock bottom here, while I'm still getting by on my low-grade irritability."

Both Anna and Bo knew exactly where it came from. There was a long line of rebels-without-a-cause in their family tree-both sides. Both their mother's and father's ancestors had raised known problem children who grew up to be problem adults. Anna and Bo weren't wildcards. Their unpredictability was predicted from early on.

Anna started crying again, this time a weepy sniffling.

"Anna, are you close to your room yet?"

"Yes," Anna coughed up in reply.

"Then I'm going to let you go. I can't help you out of this. Try calling Mary again. Or," Bo paused as she heard Anna board an elevator.

"Or what?" Anna sniveled as she pressed the button for the 12th floor.

"Why don't you go take a *real* vacation? Go home for a while. *Home* home."

CHAPTER SIX

Dutch had finished up at the work site and was on his way to collect CaitlinJo when his cell rang. It was Jody.

"Hi Jody," he muttered into the phone as he punched his turn signal and eased his foot on the break.

"Hi, boss. I checked your calendars and spoke with Jeanette. She's a talker! Anyway, it's looking like you'll be clear for the first weekend of March, which is," Jody paused for effect. "Next weekend. No family commitments that I saw in your personal calendar and no engagements for any of the ongoing projects here in town. Maplewood is yours," she sighed as though it had taken her a bit of legwork.

"Terrific, Jody. Thanks for taking a look for me. I can always count on you. I gotta grab Cait, but I'll see you at the office later today or tomorrow." Dutch hung up and swung his truck into Sonoran Country Day School's parent-pick-up loop. He threw the dusty, four-door beast into park, hopped out, and trotted up to the office.

"Daddy!" CaitlinJo squealed when she saw him from a little line of preschoolers in the adjacent hallway.

Dutch was about three minutes early, which would allow him to get in and out without having to chitchat with the stay-at-home moms who always seemed to wrangle him into submission until it was past naptime.

Not only did the moms remind him of Megan, who was a beautiful, chatty stay-at-home mom herself, but they also wore on his nerves. It was one thing to be an attentive mother. But it was another to be a bored, man-hungry woman.

Dutch knew he would never date again, but if he *did*, it sure wouldn't be a mom who sent her kid to an exclusive, private preschool and had the gall to flirt with the only dad who ever turned up. No, thank you.

"Come on, Cait, let's get outta here. We gotta get home to walk Trudy," Dutch called over to the pretty little girl as he scrawled his name on the parent pick-up clipboard.

Cait gave her teacher a pleading look before she was shooed over and into Dutch's strong arms. He waved at bubbly Miss Caroline before planting a dramatic kiss on CaitlinJo's head and tickling her mercilessly.

Dutch carried his little girl upside down until they made their way past a few oncoming moms and safely to the truck. He tucked her into her big-girl car seat and carefully pulled out of the school and toward home.

"Daddy, can I hold Trudy's leash on the walk today?"

"Yes, baby girl. You can carry the poop-slingin' bag, too," Dutch joked, bringing out Caitlin's contagious giggles.

"Ew, no! That's a boy's job!"

"That's anyone's job, little lady. Boys and girls alike have to clean up poop sometimes," he informed her, turning a silly moment into a teaching one.

"Okay, fine. But only if you take me to Pizza Plex next weekend and we can ride the go-carts after!" she cried out from the backseat.

"Oh, dang. CaitlinJo, baby, I have to go to that job in the mountains next weekend. We gotta see if Meemaw and Bumpa can take care of you and Trudy. Don't let me forget to ask."

"Nooo, Daddy! I thought you promised you were gonna stay in town forever!"

He could hear CaitlinJo's heartbreaking through her exaggeration.

"Now, I never said 'forever.' I just said that I would do my best to be here as much as possible.

"Same thing, Dad," the little girl pouted from behind. She only ever called him "Dad" when was really ticked off.

They turned into the Country Club and rolled right up to the other McCree home. Once Dutch threw the truck into park, CaitlinJo unlatched herself and wiggled her way to the door, giving Dutch little time to open it and help her out, before she bolted up the smooth driveway to the front door.

CaitlinJo pressed the doorbell half a dozen times before smearing her face against the window to the side of the door.

Dutch meandered up behind her, catching a glimpse of his mom through the window as she cracked the door open and bent low.

"Who's there?" Debbie McCree sang out teasingly.

"Meemaw, it's me, CaitlinJo!" Her worries about her dad long behind her, CaitlinJo's burst into giggles for the hundredth time that day.

"CaitlinJo? I don't know any Caitlins or any Joes? What's your last name, stranger?" Debbie knew how exactly how to tickle her only grandchild into happiness.

"It's the same as YOURS, Meemaw! McCree!"

And at that, Debbie flung the door open and wrapped the little girl in a cozy grandma hug.

"Hey, Mom," Dutch drawled as he stepped over the threshold and set down CaitlinJo's glittery pink backpack on the Saltillo tile.

"Meemaw, Daddy is leaving me." The little girl turned on a dime, releasing herself from her grandmother's hug, propping her hands on her slight hips, and pursing her mouth accusingly at Dutch.

Debbie stood and smoothed her yellow apron down, tilting her chin toward her son. "Maplewood?" she asked.

"Yep, first weekend of March. Any chance CaitlinJo and Trudy can have a sleepover?"

Debbie smiled and patted her granddaughter's dark hair, "I was actually going to ask *you* if you wanted to stay over that weekend! How perfect, darling," she cooed.

Dutch was amazed at his mother's unending warmth and cleverness. Winking at her, he squatted down to his girl.

"Baby, you two put together plans for your special weekend, and you and me can go shopping later. We can get yummy treats and maybe a new game or toy?"

A smile spread across CaitlinJo's tiny mouth. "Okay, Daddy," she replied as she fell into his arms for a goodbye hug before he had to return to work.

CHAPTER SEVEN

The night before, Anna had crawled into bed as soon as she let herself into the room she shared with Jenna. She didn't shower. She didn't even take off her makeup. And she definitely didn't text or call Jessica or Jenna or even Amber to see if everyone was okay.

Now, as she yawned herself awake in the sprawling suite, she felt a pang of guilt. She certainly wasn't being a very good friend.

She slid out of bed in her crumpled nightshirt and ambled to the living room, where she turned on the television for background noise.

Something caught her attention and she quickly clicked it back off.

Jenna wasn't in her bed. And, in fact, the queen-sized duvet and sheets were crisply tucked and untouched. She had never returned from the previous night.

Anna felt her irritation mounting. Frustrated that she had to play babysitter for once, she strode back to her bed, where she dug around in the sheets for her phone. Empty-handed, she went to the kitchen and grabbed her clutch, finding the little device there but dead. She dipped back into her room and dug through her overnight bed until she felt the tail of her charger. Thrusting the charger into the port and the plug into the nearest outlet, she went back out to the living room and the connecting door and banged on it.

"Amber, are you awake? Open up!" She called through the metal barricade.

Nothing.

She pounded again. "Amber? Jessica? Wake. Up. Please. Lord."

A second of fear fired through her body and she pressed her ear against the door, listening hard for movement or words. After a beat, she finally heard something.

Amber's muffled voice called back, "Coming!"

Relieved, Anna stood back.

"What?" After opening the door, Amber rubbed her eyes awake with one hand and stretched the other fist up and back toward the vaulted ceiling. In her pink terrycloth robe and fuzzy slippers, she looked like a Sunday morning cartoon. Of the four of them, Anna would not have expected simple Amber to overpack, but there she was: buried in a bag's worth of nightclothes and comfy-ness.

"Is Jessica in there?" Anna replied, her voice high.

Amber glanced behind her. "No, she's not back yet." She stretched again and yawned before inhaling deeply and staring back at Anna dumbly.

"It's…" Anna whipped her head back, searching the nearby kitchenette for the microwave clock. "It's seven-thirty!" She exclaimed upon seeing the time.

Amber cocked her head and set her hand on her thick waist. "So? Do you have amnesia? This is literally how it goes. Every girls' trip. Every weekend, even. You three go out. You meet guys. You show up the next morning, bedraggled and hung over."

Anna felt dizzy as if she did have amnesia.

Everything about her life for the last decade swirled like a kaleidoscope in her head. She nodded absently to Amber and invited her over to her kitchenette for coffee.

As the two sipped in silence, Anna reflected further. She felt gross. For herself and for her friends. She said as much to Amber.

"Why have you tolerated this behavior from us?"

Amber looked up from her phone, moderately surprised. "What do you mean?"

"Almost every weekend we go out and meet guys, leaving you behind as we chase... what? What are we even chasing?" Anna stared out the window at the far side of the living room.

Amber considered this before replying. "We all like to go out. There's nothing wrong with it." She stirred at her coffee aimlessly, frowning deeply.

"I get that. We like to have fun. I know. But the hookups. Like, what are we looking for? What are we getting out of it?"

Amber didn't hesitate to respond to that. "I don't hook up. Nor do I want to."

"I know, so why do you even hang out with us, Amber?"

"Jessica is my best friend and my family. Jenna, too. You're a best friend to us. And, anyway, I don't have anything else to do. And it's kinda fun to hear about what you three get yourselves into." She scooted her mug out from her spot at the table and propped her elbows where it had been. "Like, remember the last time we were in Vegas and you met those Australian guys and Jenna got a concussion? Now *that* was wild. It was better than reality T.V.!" Amber guffawed obnoxiously.

Anna didn't laugh. She did remember. It was only last fall, and she had had to make a decision on whether to call a dang ambulance. Fortunately, Jenna woke up, and she and Anna returned, relatively unscathed.

But now, half-a-year later she was feeling very scathed. Anna wasn't raised like that. Setting aside the question of whether it was right or wrong to go to a stranger's hotel room, she had always known it was not *safe*.

And yet for the last decade or more, she had done just that. Not *every* weekend. Not *every* guy. Mostly the girls would go out, grab a few drinks, flirt, and be on their merry way. But there had been lots of kissing strangers. Lots of broken promises that those strangers would call. Lots of nothing.

Amber was back to scrolling through her phone and slurping away at her sugary coffee. Anna thought of Mary and how she never got through to her youngest sister the night before.

She twisted in her chair toward the kitchen bar and tugged her phone from the charger. It had turned on, finally, and was flashing new messages and a missed call and voicemail.

One text from Roberta: *Checking in. Did you survive the night?*

One text from Mary: *Sorry I missed your call! Kurt's visiting this weekend...*

One call and voicemail from Jenna and Jessica, who were singing sloppily into her inbox that they were grabbing breakfast in the hotel bar. Which hotel bar, Anna didn't care to know.

"They're alive," Anna announced to Amber as soon as she deleted the ugly voicemail.

Amber didn't look up, but instead slurped her coffee once more before muttering, "Who?"

Anna opened her mouth to slam Amber for her indifferent attitude. But, she stopped.

Instead, she pushed herself up from the table, leaving her phone there, and slowly walked to the bathroom. Once inside, she gently closed the door and turned the shower on until it was steaming. Before she got in, she caught her reflection in the golden-framed mirror. Pausing there, above the marble countertop, she saw someone she didn't know anymore.

CHAPTER EIGHT

Dutch straightened from his sink and dabbed a hand towel across his freshly shaven face. His mom had already come to collect CaitlinJo, which gave him enough time to shower and shave before heading up to the mountains.

His meeting with Michael Erinhard was slated for that afternoon. Jeannette had made arrangements for the two men to have dinner afterward at the supposed best steakhouse on the mountain, Jake's Steaks.

He finished getting ready, grabbed his overnight bag, loaded up in the truck and took the back way to Maplewood.

The drive up the mountain was slow-going, so Dutch punched the radio on, picking up a country station here and Christian Talk Radio there. He settled in and tried to enjoy himself, reflecting on his various building contracts.

Try as he might, his attitude slipped. Every other project was on track and manageable. But, Dutch had started to regret the Maplewood Luxury Cabins. The long drive coupled with weekends away from CaitlinJo had begun to eat at him. He was a homebody, by nature. One-vacation-a-year-max type of person. And that vacation was almost always to a sunny Mexican beach.

Still, he appreciated certain things about Maplewood. He liked the slow pace of life and the small-town folk. They seemed to cling to values that weren't so common in the big city. Dutch went back and forth on whether he would end up securing himself one of the cabins as a vacation home. His friends and parents all thought he needed to. It would give him a personal retreat and CaitlinJo future opportunities. She could learn to ski or snowboard one day. But his heart was lazy and stubborn. He couldn't picture himself changing his routine so much.

And, anyway, he liked being near his parents, who were well-cemented in their Scottsdale hamlet. Debbie had her book club and her Bunco group. She swam with Linda and Lela at the pool every Tuesday and Thursday. William Senior, or "Bill," McCree had Knights of Columbus obligations and a weekly poker game with the guys from Rotary Club. They kept to their routines, too. No traveling for them. Almost ever.

Slowly, the barren landscape grew like a hand-drawn cartoon. Dirt and cactus turning to low brush turning to spindly trees. Finally, as he passed through the canyon, the truck became submerged in green. It really was a wonder. He could travel from desert to forest in less than four hours.

He whizzed through thick and looming pine and oak. Little patches of snow began to peek out from under periodic maple trees and aspens. It was amazing to him that there was still a bit of snow up there.

At last, Dutch passed the little gas station at the fork and headed another mile down the road until he turned right onto Pine Burst Lane. He noted that landscaping was coming along nicely. Saplings lined the main drive.

He had his men begin the whole project with the gates. It seemed silly and impractical, but Michael and even Jeanette argued that the gates would tell the community that this place was exclusive. It would set a *tone*, they said.

He tapped in his code and waited for the iron and wood gates to swing back, inviting him in. Each time he came to town, Jeanette told him he could stay with her and her boyfriend, Garold. But he'd rather hole up in one of the model units than infringe on their privacy. Fortunately, he found a little motel down the road and stayed there for each trip. He was a simple guy with simple tastes, after all.

He turned left after the gate into the parking lot of the clubhouse, where the development's offices were housed. Two cars had beat him there.

Michael was standing outside the pine entry doors, his arms crossed in front of his North Face pullover as he appeared to listen intently to an animated Jeanette.

Dutch threw the truck in park and hopped out. He'd worn a flannel button-down and jeans, his usual work uniform. Sometimes he'd trade the flannel for an Oxford, but it was rare. He pushed his dark blonde hair back from his forehead and strode up to the steps, first saying hello to Jeanette with a generous smile and nod and then offering a hearty handshake to Michael.

"Mike, before we even do a walk-through, I want to talk demographics and projections. Jeanette, did you pull that info for us?" Dutch turned all business, which seemed to excite Jeanette, who matched his tone and immediately directed the men inside and into her temporary office.

Michael started the conversation before the three sat down in the pinewood office. "I took the liberty of digging around myself," he launched. "Jeanette's figures agree with my anecdotal evidence that Maplewood is on the brink of some significant growth."

"What kind of growth, and what's the source? I've wondered since we started this project exactly what industry serves the mountain, other than modest tourism," Dutch took control of the conversation, his deep voice dominating.

Jeanette's excitement turned to fluster as she shuffled papers on the desk.

Michael answered, his voice even. "I'm surprised you haven't heard, William." Dutch cringed at the use of his given name.

"Call me Dutch, Mike," he interjected.

"Dutch… I'm surprised you haven't heard about the hospital. Greater Maplewood Mountain has signed into a community partnership with a national network of healthcare providers *and* research universities." He sounded like a television commercial. "They are starting construction on a regional healthcare facility to include everything from complete emergency services to a neonatal intensive care unit to a cancer research facility. It's big news around these parts." Michael let the smugness in his voice ooze over the last sentence.

Dutch could have kicked himself, but then he remembered: he wasn't from *these parts*. He considered saying as much but thought better of it. This hospital *was* excellent news. "Wow," Dutch replied, a grin creeping up his rugged face, crinkling the corners of his ice-blue eyes. "This is extremely promising. I can't believe I was so out of the loop. Please, continue," he prompted as he locked eyes with a flushed Jeanette.

CHAPTER NINE

Anna had spent the next half-an-hour showering and scrubbing her face and hair and body as thoroughly as she possibly could with her travel-sized shampoo and body wash bottles. When her skin was practically raw, she stepped out, dried herself off, wrapped her hair in the towel, and brushed her teeth. She then stepped into her airplane outfit- a tracksuit. Instead of makeup, she slathered on her sunscreen-laden moisturizer and rubbed Chapstick over her full, naked lips. That was it. She wanted a blank canvas for Sunday.

When she opened the bathroom door and let the steam streak through the suite, she saw that Jenna had returned. Her clutch and dress were strewn across the bed. Her heels splayed on the floor below.

Anna moved into the kitchenette, where Jenna was nursing a mug of coffee, her makeup somewhat still in place but her hair flat and tired. She didn't look up.

"How was your night?" Anna felt her mother's voice in her own, a thin layer of guilt nearly imperceptible.

"Oh, you know. Same old, same old," Jenna chuckled as she lowered the mug to answer, her smeared lips curling into a smile. "How come you bailed?" Her left penciled eyebrow arched scornfully up toward Anna.

Anna felt herself recoil slightly before answering, her voice bitter. "I dunno, Jen. I guess it's starting to get old, you know?" She pulled out the adjacent chair and propped her elbow atop the table, resting her chin in her hand.

Jenna steadied her gaze on Anna. "Not really. Are you becoming an old lady now that you're in your thirties?" Her laugh was sincere.

Anna thought back to her shower and her earlier conversation with Amber. She'd come to a couple realizations.

One: she didn't want to party anymore. She needed a break. Her body needed a break. Her soul needed a break.

Two: she didn't want to date or see any guys anymore. Maybe forever. She knew she'd never find what Mary had found in Kurt. She missed that opportunity if there ever was one.

Three: For the first time in her adult life, Anna was homesick.

The third revelation was most shocking to her. As she stood in the shower, letting the falling water wrap her in its warmth, she realized that her lifestyle was not late-stage teenage rebellion. It was much deeper.

But she still had a strong urge to go home and hunker down in the bed she'd shared with Bo or pull a barstool up to the kitchen counter and breathe in her mom's baking. She'd even be willing to milk the cows again or forage for eggs in the coop in the wee hours of the morning just to have the hug of home around her body.

Suddenly, she felt tears prick at the corners of her eyes.

She stabbed at her eyes and rose from the table in a sudden, jerking movement.

"Yeah, something like that," she answered Jenna before storming back to the room and slipping beneath the covers of the side of the bed she hadn't slept on the night before.

Anna pulled her phone up to her face and navigated to Mary's text. Her manicured fingers snapped out a quick, belated reply.

I want to come home.

CHAPTER TEN

Dutch and Michael had finished walking the property and driving the perimeter within an hour and had settled into a booth in the dimly lit dining room of Jake's. Dutch hadn't yet been there, and he was admiring the cattle hide lining of the seat backs, the antler chandeliers, and an impressive trophy wall which boasted beasts of every kind.

When he was younger, his father would take him hunting each year. They'd have the meat processed and frozen, and they would store it for the winter. His parents fully believed in sustainability before it was a pop-culture trend.

However, his family's hunter and gatherer days were long gone. Now, his folks were content to sit in an air-conditioned stucco-framed country-club home and eat microwavable t.v. dinners twice a day.

As he sat in the authentic steakhouse, Dutch realized he sort of missed the good old days of chopping firewood and picking those nasty Bisbee burrs out of his jeans. Life had gotten a little too comfortable for Dutch McCree.

Once the waiter had taken their drink orders – whiskey neat for Dutch, margarita for Michael – they took back up their conversation.

"So, it's looking like a 'go,' then?" Michael laced his fingers atop the table and leaned forward, his eyebrows furrowed.

Dutch didn't hesitate. Jeanette's paperwork and Michael's own research had proved his case. "Definitely. If the hospital is breaking ground within the next couple weeks or months, we might even see some early buyers. I'd think the real estate market up here is going to start sizzling."

"I agree. Once I read about the hospital, I immediately called Jeanette and had her start reaching out to council members and real estate agents to get more info. Everything is coming together nicely. I'm really glad to be part of the process. It's not often that architects get to be so hands-on from start to finish with projects like this one."

Dutch smiled warmly at him. "I'm glad to have you on board, too." He felt an early friendship taking shape as the two discussed their families and hobbies. He learned that Michael had two children, a boy and girl, and lived in a similar development to his, but in Mesa. The drive into Maplewood was significantly shorter for Michael.

"There is no doubt I will buy a cabin in the development," Michael admitted. "I would love to teach Scott and Katie to ski, and Kara would love it up here. I can just picture her in a little snow bunny outfit, reading a book in the ski lodge," Michael continued.

Dutch was a little taken aback at how comfortable and open Michael was. His love and affection for his wife were palpable.

Dutch's eyes began to water, suddenly. He cleared his throat to push away the sadness. He had long ago accepted Megan's passing and felt that he had truly come to terms with it. Yes, he often missed her and thought of her. But these days, he pinned his melancholy not on the fact that he had lost his wife but that CaitlinJo had lost her mother. He worried about it all the damn time. Mostly, he worried because he knew he could never give CaitlinJo what *she* needed. He simply wasn't able.

Their steaks had arrived, and Michael was sawing away as he carried the conversation. "So, Dutch, are you going to buy in the Cabins?" Sometimes, Michael shortened the name to just the Cabins, which Dutch thought was a trendy thing to do, but he didn't mind.

"I hadn't planned on it, really," Dutch started, before taking a bite of the tender, pink meat. He chased the savory chunk with a sip of his drink as he waited for Michael to respond.

"Yeah, I hear ya. I'm going to see how it takes shape, too. I feel that while you can plan a housing development, you can never quite predict the dynamics of a *neighborhood*."

Dutch liked that. It was true. In all his years of building houses, he learned one thing: Location. Location. Location. A beautiful, million-dollar home wouldn't stand a chance at reselling if a Laundromat popped up next door. Of course, a planned community such as Maplewood Luxury Cabins wouldn't have that issue. It was gated, for goodness sake. But, who knew how the land around the property would develop? And what types of people would end up purchasing? Second-home owners from the valley? Doctors from the new hospital? Locals? For some reason, he couldn't imagine rural-type folks having an interest in the "Cabins." But, who knew?

"So," Michael continued between bites, "Are you thinking of going out while you're up here? I'm not one to go out myself, especially since I have Kara with me, but I hear there is a neat little bar up the mountain. And, besides, country girls can be pretty fun."

Dutch cocked a brow at Michael before quickly replying, "Heck, no."

CHAPTER ELEVEN

Monday had finally rolled around, and Anna was thankful to be back at the office. Despite her exhaustion, she still managed to make it in on time and without issue. No one ever suspected how she spent her weekends, not even her boss, Kurt Cutler.

But she knew exactly how he had spent his weekend.

Anna and her youngest sister, Mary, talked for a while before she left Vegas. Anna heard all about how they cooked together, played card games, went for walks in the chilly Maplewood evenings. She and Kurt had been dating since December, but things seemed to be moving in a serious direction quickly. Anna knew this because Mary had never brought a boyfriend home. But, Kurt had been invited to the family Christmas dinner just two months ago and almost immediately after they had first met.

Anna stole a glance at Kurt as she glided over to her desk.

Although she didn't exactly have a type, Kurt really wasn't it. He was a little too much of a nice guy for her taste.

Anna shook her head to herself, reminding herself that as of this weekend- no more guys. No more dates. No more clubs. No more parties with the girls.

In fact, the flight home with her friends had been a step in the right direction: awkward. Anna made it clear that there had been a shift in her interests. The others didn't believe it or didn't want to hear it, because they ignored her the rest of the way home.

Now, as she booted up her computer and clicked awake her phone, she felt a renewed focus. Drawing a sip from her espresso, Anna felt the smooth velvety liquid coat the light breakfast she'd enjoyed after a quick session on her in-home treadmill that morning.

She was officially turning over a new leaf. It may be two months into the New Year, but she was beginning her resolution now.

Just as she clicked into her email, a new one popped up. It was from Bo. Anna had sent her a long, sappy message about sisterhood and family the night before, while she was still reeling from her weekend away.

Don't go overboard. Stay you, woman.

Anna smiled at her computer screen. But, her smiled faded as she watched Kurt saunter over to her desk. He rarely paid her little visits to the office. Things had become a little more professional between them. Well, they had always been professional, but now even more so. He acted like he was overcompensating for dating her sister.

"Anna, good morning!" He cheered at her above his coffee mug.

She let herself smile back. She really did like Kurt, as a person.

"Hi, boss. What can I do ya for?" She cringed at the lame line. "What's up?"

Kurt chuckled. "I would love a chance to talk with you about a new idea I have for the company. Are you up for a stroll?"

Because of their open-office design, privacy did not exist at FantasyCoin, the fantasy sports/cryptocurrency tech company where Anna was Vice President. She, herself, had been the one to weigh in on the design aspects, but sometimes she regretted going with the trends. There was no alone time, even when she had her headphones in and was completely zoned into her computer.

So, whenever Kurt wanted to talk company politics or ethics or Big Decisions, he would ask her to go to the separate lunch room on their floor or for a walk- to get away from the rest of the staff, comprised modestly of a couple coders, a marketing expert, and some general operations guys.

"Sure," Anna replied. Her interest was piqued. The company had been surprised to find themselves continuing on in their success. There was a bit of a dip in the market just before Christmas, as there was across almost all blockchain-based projects, but FantasyCoin had made it through to January nicely ahead of the curve. Once football season had ended with the Superbowl, they had steadied themselves for another drop by releasing a new app for Fantasy Basketball just in time for March Madness. They were smart and kept themselves relevant in the off-season by over-developing the blockchain and investment deals and rolling out Fantasy apps for every pro sport they could think of.

Anna couldn't imagine what Kurt had in mind. Business was stable. Stable was good.

Once they had breezed through the front doors of the office building and into the warm Phoenix air, Kurt dropped it on her.

"Expansion," he said.

"As in? Bigger office? More staff?" Anna was confused; they were working comfortably within their operations budget without forcing any overtime.

Kurt took his hand out of his pocket and waved it in front of them as they walked the sidewalk in a loop around the towering Downtown building. "No, no, no. Well, not really. I mean geographically. Opening a satellite office," he finished and slowed to watch her reaction.

"To where? Silicon Valley? It's expensive Kurt, and probably unnecessary," Anna began in on what had become a back-and-forth discussion on relocating to California in order to meld with the mainstream tech community.

Kurt's pace quickened again. "Nope, not at all. I'm talking more locally." He then paused and opened to face her, flashing a bright smile. She was stumped.

"Tucson?" She said, before giving up and dropping her open hands to her sides, her face a question mark.

"Maplewood," he finally answered, his eyes filled with a secret. "I'm going to have to live closer to your sister if I plan to propose to her, after all."

CHAPTER TWELVE

"A re you staying over tonight or heading back down the mountain?" Michael asked Dutch once they'd paid their bills and stood to leave.

"Down the mountain at night? Not a chance. I'll stay over and leave after breakfast. You?" Dutch stretched his long torso from side to side before leading the way to the exit.

"Actually, my family joined me for this trip. It was the only way I could convince Kara to let me come up to talk shop again. She's getting sick of the business travel."

"Oh? Don't tell me Jeanette's putting you up? That could be cramped," Dutch joked.

"No, actually we found a rustic bed-and-breakfast-type joint a little farther up the mountain. It's great. Wood Smoke Lodge. Ever heard of it?"

Dutch shook his head no. It sounded nicer than the dumpy little motel, but he had no interest in traveling deeper into town. He wanted to get back on the road to greet CaitlinJo by the time she woke up from her midday nap.

"Well, on your next trip you should check it out. The innkeeper is very cool. I hear she makes a mean flapjack, so I'm looking forward to breakfast with the fam."

Dutch stifled a laugh at Michael's attempt at down-home slang. Although, talk of flapjacks and a lodge in the woods did sound appealing. Still, he shook it off and said his farewell to Michael. The two agreed to touch base on what they were now calling "Phase II" by Monday.

Dutch made his way back past the fork and pulled his truck into the little motel parking lot. After checking in, he grabbed his overnight bag out of the truck and stepped up to room number one, just next door to the front office.

He felt anxious, though he couldn't put his finger on it. Other than staying over in a questionable motel, everything else was smooth sailing in his life. This extension project looked great and would likely net him more income than he had planned. CaitlinJo was soaring in preschool. His parents were happy. Even little Trudy the Chihuahua seemed healthy.

Maybe it was just being away from home, but Dutch tossed and turned all night.

Finally, at what must have been around four o'clock in the morning, he fell asleep and slept hard. So hard, that he didn't hear his six o'clock alarm go off and almost missed a third phone call at nine o'clock. By the time he groggily swiped the phone to answer, the caller had hung up. Just as he dropped the phone on the bed and turned to catch another few minutes of shuteye, his text notification chirped loudly.

Call me when you can- if you haven't left town yet. Urgent. —Michael

Chapter Thirteen

Anna was in shock. She hadn't seen any of this coming. It was early. And, Kurt? Really? He was divorced and career-focused and a city-boy. He couldn't possibly be serious about Maplewood. She did a mental catalog of all the reasons it would make no sense for Kurt to propose to Mary.

But then again, it was very apparent that he was serious about her sister. And, she knew Mary was very serious about him, despite their different backgrounds.

Anna listened on as Kurt, uncharacteristically, went into details about how he loved her sister and saw a future with her and out of the big city.

The biggest problem was that Mary was unable to relocate her business, the Lodge, to Phoenix. And would she want to? And would he even want her to?

A better idea, he thought, was opening up a satellite office in Maplewood and reducing his own commitments to the company. He wanted Anna to take on a bigger role to fill his absence but allow him to be an equal player still.

Co-presidents of FantasyCoin, he offered.

Anna was beside herself with anticipation and excitement and nerves. At first, when he pitched the Mary thing, her heart sank a little. Just as she was writing off relationships, her baby sister was about to embark on the most important relationship of her life. It hurt, a little.

But when Kurt turned the conversation in this unprecedented direction, her new-found focus and confidence from that morning resurfaced. She felt great. And she was completely on board. Not only because of her own promotion but because she trusted that Kurt and Mary were going to make it as a couple.

Seeing their chemistry at Christmastime was equal parts nauseating and inspiring. And to hear Kurt talk about her now, Anna knew that he loved her sister. And listening to Mary yesterday, she knew Mary loved him back. Deeply. It may be soon, but it was right.

The only problem would be the logistics of setting up shop in Maplewood.

"How soon are we talking? By summer?" She asked him.

"Now. I'm ready to do this. I don't want to wait. I was planning on going back to Maplewood this weekend. While I'm there, I'm going to take a look at office spaces."

Anna thought for a moment as they continued their loop around the building.

"No," she started. Kurt paused in his pace and tilted his head.

"No?"

"No, I mean- it's all terrific, of course. Very exciting. But Maplewood? The electricity goes out once per month. You can imagine how phones and internet work. It's not conducive to a tech-focused business." She furrowed her brow as she continued brainstorming. Kurt kept quiet, allowing her to process. "Lowell is like half an hour from the Lodge. It's still technically on the mountain, but I know it has a better infrastructure. Outages are rare and phone service is better. It'd be a safer bet. If you're serious, we can go together and make appointments to look around," she finished.

Kurt grinned widely. "That's why I hired you, Anna," he put his hand on her shoulder. "You don't beat around the bush. You get things done."

Weakly, she smiled back and then continued on in finishing the loop to head back inside. But as she walked next to him, a worry caught in her heart. Was she really worthy of this promotion? Or was Kurt promoting her because it suited his plans to move? She bit down on her lip before realizing she was all but sprinting. She had moved ahead of Kurt by ten yards.

She turned her head back to see him smiling down at his phone.

Anna began to roll her eyes at his puppy-dog affection for Mary, but something stopped her.

She realized it didn't matter why Kurt was promoting her. She was good enough for it, and that's why he was comfortable doing it. What mattered most was happiness. But what she was feeling right then was not happiness for herself, so much. It was happiness for her sister. Anna was happy that her sister had found someone who loved her as much as Kurt did. Someone who was willing to give up his world for hers.

She allowed herself to smile, instead, as she pulled open the doors and walked into the building before riding up the elevator to their offices. *Her* offices.

And yet, the corners of her mouth pulled down when she walked inside and still felt a tug on her heart.

***

Four days later, they decided to leave together just before lunch so that they could make it up the mountain before nightfall. It was Friday, and traffic would be awful if they waited until the afternoon.

Since they took Kurt's car, Anna spent the ride making phone calls around Lowell. She successfully scheduled four showings for small office spaces around town. But as they discussed the matter further, it became clear that they had better not rule out Maplewood. After all, Kurt could work from home, if need be. Cell coverage was good enough to make up for internet outages or the like.

Of course, that created the question of where, exactly, Kurt would live. He insisted that he could stay at the Lodge with Mary until they figured out where to go next.

But, Anna knew her sister better than that. As they cruised through green pine trees and oaks that were just now coming back to life as winter began to fade, Anna rolled her eyes and stifled a chuckle. Anna may be stubborn, but Mary Delaney had morals.

"Kurt, you are definitely going to have to find somewhere else to live," Anna said as he pulled the car off Maplewood Boulevard and down the gravelly, aspen-studded drive of Wood Smoke Lodge.

CHAPTER FOURTEEN

Dutch rolled out of bed into a quick stretch before pulling off his white t-shirt and heading toward the bathroom, phone in hand.

As he walked over to the little sink to fill one of the plastic coffee cups with stale motel water, he swiped over to Michael's phone number and clicked *Call*.

Michael picked up on the first ring. "Dutch, are you on the road yet?" His voice was excited.

"Nope, I overslept. Getting ready to head out now. I'll grab some breakfast on the road," Dutch examined himself in the fuzzy mirror, taking in his five o'clock shadow and dirty blonde bedhead.

"Excellent! Okay, real quick," Michael broke into a sales pitch, explaining to Dutch that he and his wife and kids were enjoying a scrumptious breakfast of crispy bacon and pancakes (which did nothing but make Dutch kick himself for choosing the low-budget, no-tell motel with a questionable front desk clerk).

"Sorry, Mike, but, ah, can you get to the point? I'm really hoping to get going soon," Dutch interjected as he pulled clean boxers, a fresh flannel shirt, and an extra pair of jeans from his bag and laid them across the bed.

"So, long story short, there is a gentleman here who is hoping to take a tour of the building site and maybe scope out a floor plan or model cabin. I thought it'd be a great chance for you to," Michael paused, then lowered his voice, "you know, help make an early sale. Get things rolling ahead of schedule."

Dutch thought about it for a moment. There was nothing he would do differently than Jeanette or a realtor or even

Michael, really. He didn't understand why he needed to stick around to show some "buyer" a home. It wasn't his job.

"I don't know, Mike. Can you do it? Or maybe Jeanette is up for working a Saturday?" He squeezed some paste onto his toothbrush and continued his routine as he waited for Michael's reply, which seemed to come after further, hushed discussion with the other company at the Lodge.

As he listened in on muffled back-and-forth, a text message popped up on his phone. It was from his mom.

Dutch, have you left? If not, take your time. Cait wants to stay here again tonight. Too much fun at Meemaw and Bumpa's house! LOL ☺

Dutch smiled. Despite her age and stubbornness, his mom had adapted quite nicely to texting. He knew he should get off the phone with Michael and call CaitlinJo to see if it was true. But something nagged at him.

"Hey, Dutch," Michael came back on and seemed to have found a quiet place to talk. "You can take off if you really need to. I've got this. I only ask you, because this potential buyer is *Kurt Cutler*!" Michael's voice rose in excitement.

Dutch didn't understand. "Who?"

"You know, the Phoenix tech dude. He's like a local Steve Jobs. He's revolutionized the tech industry in Downtown Phoenix. I cannot believe you haven't heard of him."

Dutch had never heard of him and was now even more annoyed.

"Nope, doesn't ring a bell." Dutch spat out the rest of his toothpaste and set the phone on speaker as he began to strip out of his boxers.

"Allow me to enlighten you. Kurt Cutler could be an excellent asset as we enter the initial selling phase. He has contacts all over Arizona, regionally, even nationally. There is only one spot for him in this tiny little town, and it's got to be our development. He says he wants to take a close look, because the home may double as a satellite office." Michael's excitement was hardly contagious, but Dutch appreciated how much he cared about the project. He swiped back to his mom's text, thinking about CaitlinJo playing cards with her grandparents, taking little Trudy on a walk, eating cookies and milk.

"Fine, sure," he replied, at last, eyeing the shower. "When do you wanna meet?"

"Terrific," Michael replied. "We can be down there within an hour."

Dutch sighed, accepting that it was a smart move. "Okay, see ya at the office."

"Oh, and Dutch," Michael continued, "He's bringing a woman with him, but she's not his girlfriend or wife or anything like that."

"Okay?" Dutch scratched his head as he turned the hot water faucet on max.

"She's, well, she's…" Michael trailed off, and Dutch could hear his muffled voice mix with a woman's. "You'll want to look presentable," he finished before hanging up on Dutch.

He felt his chest tighten slightly as he grabbed the phone to text his mom back.

That's perfect… because something has come up.

CHAPTER FIFTEEN

"He'll meet us there," Michael announced to the small group as he reentered the dining room from the back deck.

"Meet who where?" Mary replied as she strode from the kitchen to sweep up the syrup-glued plates and empty coffee mugs.

Anna's eyes darted from her sister's face to Kurt's. Kurt hadn't yet made clear to the architect that he distinctly did not want to share this plan with his innkeeper girlfriend.

Just as Michael was about to fill Mary in, Kurt cleared his throat. Glancing sharply at Michael, he answered her. "Michael mentioned a potential *office space* available not too far from his development. He thought we should check it out and set up an appointment with the leasing agent." Kurt stumbled through the fib, and Anna couldn't stifle a small smile.

She knew Mary was smart as a whip, but would her naïve sister accept Kurt's half-truth or put two and two together?

"In town?" Mary eyed the handsome tech-genius suspiciously.

"Yeah, well," Kurt looked down at his watch. "Mary, I know you have other guests to prep for, we shouldn't be long. I'll give you a call when we're on our way back up," he finished without meeting her eye and started out of the dining room.

Anna felt Mary's eyes shift to her face. She shrugged. "Business trip, Mare."

Michael's wife and kids were squabbling over how they would occupy themselves as Michael added an unexpected errand to their vacation. Anna felt Mary move behind her and poke her in the back.

"Can I talk to you privately for a moment?"

"Sure," Anna replied coolly. She honestly didn't know what Kurt had in mind. Once Michael had started pitching his luxury cabins community, it was obvious what Kurt was thinking... but he didn't even have an office, yet. Anna figured he'd broach the topic of moving into the Lodge, not the idea of buying a home in Maplewood.

"What's going on?" Mary's voice was filled with irritation and accusation- in equal measure.

"I have no idea, Mare," Anna answered once they were safely tucked into the reception area beyond the great room.

"Did you put Kurt up to that?"

"Up to what?"

"Last night he brought up the idea of moving in together. You know how I feel about that," Mary chastised, propping her hand on her hip.

"Yes, and I warned him," Anna responded, bored.

"So, then, why is he moving forward with looking at office spaces if he doesn't have a place to live?"

Anna stalled, uncertain how best to proceed. She thought for a moment about her sister's question and nearly started in on ridiculing Mary for her old-fashioned values and prudishness. It came naturally to Anna to question Mary's seemingly-out-dated morals and to put her little sister in the position of defending herself against Anna's self-righteous attitude.

But, she stopped herself. She neither defended Kurt's desire to move things along nor did she push Mary out of her comfort zone. Instead, she offered a reasonable and truthful answer.

"Mary, I think he just loves you. He's trying to lay some groundwork here. So why don't you finish up clearing for breakfast and turning the beds for tonight. I'll go with Kurt and be your advocate." Anna didn't hear her usual self in her voice, but she liked the difference.

Mary didn't seem to notice Anna's shift. She pinched her eyebrows together and let her gaze follow Michael and his bubbly family as they moved from the dining room and up to the guest rooms.

"Be back down in just a minute!" He cheerily called over his shoulder as he pressed his hand into his wife's lower back and guided her up the pine-railed staircase.

Anna wondered what Kara Erinhard and the kids would do while she and Kurt stole Michael to take a look at the Cabins, as he called them.

As if reading her mind, Mary chimed in, "Snowshoeing. That's what we'll do. I just bought a few pairs when they went on sale after New Year's. I bet the kids will get a kick out of it. There's just enough snow to allow for a quick jaunt."

Anna cocked her eyebrow. There was little snow at the Lodge. It had begun to melt a week earlier. Yes, it was still chilly, but the ground was mostly just slush.

"Up towards the ski hill there's more; I promise you. I'll keep the Erinhards busy. You help Kurt do whatever he needs to." Mary winked at her, and Anna felt impressed by Mary's easy trust.

"We'll see you later then," she replied, grabbing her coat from the rack and pulling it on. Just as Michael and Kurt appeared on the landing above, Mary grabbed Anna's wrist and pulled her into the kitchen.

"What is it?" Anna asked, worry pinching her face.

"Ann, what if he proposes?" Mary's eyes were on fire, and her lips spread into a hopeful smile. But Anna was taken off-guard.

"Well, don't you want that?" Was all she could offer as a reply.

"But what if he doesn't ask Dad? Or he expects me to move in with him after proposing but before marriage? Or?" Mary's smile waned as she waited for Anna to comfort her.

But Anna couldn't do that. She could only be honest. "Mary, do you *know* Kurt?"

Mary didn't hesitate. "I know he loves me."

Anna tucked a strand of Mary's wild chestnut hair behind her ear and replied, "Then you take that love and you give it back. And that's all you can do."

CHAPTER SIXTEEN

Dutch pulled his truck past the gate and into the office parking lot. He had beat Michael and the interested party. The parking lot was empty. Jeanette had the day off.

Dutch jumped out of the truck and strode into the office with his master key. Inside, he quickly adjusted the thermostat to a comfortable temperature and organized a few stacks of paper and errant pencils on Jeanette's desk before finding the model keys locked securely in the office closet.

He then positioned himself in the common area, leaning back onto the leather couch, his worn jeans creasing into his hip as he crossed his muscled arms over his chest. He'd silently thanked his own forethought at being sure to pack a decent outfit- an ironed, red flannel, his favorite jeans, and his non-work cowboy boots. He had a little more than a five o'clock shadow, but he figured that in small-town USA, a little stubble would be welcome.

He felt at home enough in Maplewood, where his sun-tanned face and dark-blonde hair allowed him to blend in with the locals. Michael Erinhard, despite his designer studs, also fit in, generally, for an architect.

Dutch had learned early on that Maplewood types were down-home, salt-of-the-earth, no-nonsense. He liked that.

Just as he stretched out his wrist in front of him to check the time, the wooden front door swung open. In walked Michael, ahead of a couple. Michael began in on introductions, but Dutch was distracted by the woman.

Tall and slender, she breezed through the door behind Michael and stepped up next to him to take her place directly in front of Dutch. Her wavy, reddish hair glowed against smooth, creamy skin. Green eyes flashed behind long, dark lashes. Her full, red lips were moving, and Dutch felt himself flush at the realization she was talking to him.

"And my name is Anna Delaney. I'm co-president of FantasyCoin," she finished, holding his gaze steadily.

Dutch glanced to the man behind her. Husband? Boyfriend? Fiancé? Didn't Michael say something about this? Dutch couldn't remember. But they didn't fit together. He stood awkwardly to her side, his eyes combing the high ceilings and the leather furniture around them.

Dutch noticed that she had stuck her hand out to him. He pushed off the sofa and took it in his. Her manicured fingernails contrasted by his rough, oversized hand.

"Dutch McCree, pleasure's all mine," he drawled, locking eyes with her before throwing a sidelong glance at the dark-haired man to her left. "And this must be..." he trailed off, waiting for the beautiful Anna to introduce her fellow.

The clean-shaven business type settled his gaze on Dutch. His expression was warm and open, which made Dutch uneasy for some reason.

"I'm Kurt Cutler, great to meet you, Dutch," he replied, offering his hand for a firm shake.

Dutch sized him up further as the two jogged their hands briskly. So *this* was the tech nerd Michael was talking about. He didn't look much like a computer geek to Dutch. He was well-built and dressed nicely but not like a stiff. He seemed... likable.

Then something occurred to Dutch. He'd almost missed it, but it bounced back to his mind.

"Ah, so you two work together, then?"

"Yes," Kurt answered. "I founded FantasyCoin almost two years ago and brought Anna on board right away. I recently promoted her to run the business in Phoenix. That will allow me to make the move to Maplewood, as Michael might have mentioned."

"Why Maplewood? I mean I heard about the hospital, but is there a tech revolution coming to town, too?" Dutch chuckled as he glanced over to Michael, who seemed to be growing impatient.

"This is where my girlfriend lives," Kurt corrected. "Hopefully, she'll be my fiancée soon enough." Dutch noticed Kurt flash a grin to Anna, and he felt his heart sink slightly.

"Oh, congratulations are in order, then?" Dutch's eyes darted between the two.

"Oh no," the woman threw her hair back over her shoulders dramatically, laughing at Dutch and taking a step closer to him. He felt himself lean back onto the sofa. "He's talking about my sister, Mary. She lives here. We were raised in Maplewood. But like Kurt said, in case you weren't listening, I'm in Phoenix, where I live *alone*." Her eyes narrowed on him and her lips pursed. Anna's tone was cutting, which confused him. Dutch's stomach flipped.

"I live in the valley, too, actually," he replied, licking his lips nervously.

Her eyebrow cocked, and she shifted her weight onto one hip, where she placed her long, painted fingers.

"So, Dutch McCree, it sounds like we have something in common."

CHAPTER SEVENTEEN

They had finally broken out of the clubhouse and were climbing into a jacked-up, four-door *beast* of a truck.

Anna could kick herself. She saw a hot guy and instantly fell into her old pattern. She couldn't control it.

Dutch McCree was a certified stud. She was shocked to hear he was a Phoenix boy. He looked like a homegrown Maplewood quarterback.

Or maybe a tight end. She stifled a giggle.

His boyish blonde hair that paired with crystalline blue eyes and deeply tanned skin would have made him a God among men in the sleepy little town, but he'd still fit right in. The blue jeans, the flannel, the cowboy boots, and the two-day stubble. Anna bit down on her lip to keep from saying anything else.

As soon as she heard herself utter those final, fateful words, she could feel the heat of Michael's *and* Kurt's eyes on her, amazed, no doubt, at her brazen flirting. Maybe mortified, too.

But Dutch didn't even flinch. Instead, he returned her serve with professionalism and redirection and pointed them outside to join him for a ride.

It hurt. Anna felt like a wounded deer, but she refused to act like it.

Instead, she listened in on the men's conversation, waiting for an opening.

"Maplewood Luxury Cabins currently offers 70 home sites, but Michael and I have just given the green light on a second phase. We'll expand to around 100, thanks to news of the regional medical center," Dutch droned on.

Michael jumped in, talking a mile a minute. "Mr. Cutler, I'm actually a crypto investor myself, and I have even dabbled in FantasyCoin. But, I don't know much about the day-to-day operations of a tech company such as yours. You mentioned you may be looking for an in-home office? I'd want to make sure you're aware of, well," Michael paused for a breath and took time to think of how he was going to break the news. But he didn't have to.

Anna took over for him. "Kurt is well aware of the lack of infrastructure on the Mountain. His needs will include high-speed cable internet, undoubtedly. And a phone line. But he won't be running a server here or handling any of the operating aspects. If we decide to move in that direction, we will look at office space down in Lowell, of course." She crossed her arms over her chest and leveled her gaze on Dutch, whose muscled forearms flexed as he turned the steering wheel left onto a small lane.

Dutch avoided glancing at her and instead looked ahead as he replied, "I would assume Lowell has far more in the way of luxury home opportunities, too."

Michael cleared his throat.

Anna felt Kurt lean forward behind her.

"To be clear, Lowell is not the first choice for my living arrangements," Kurt offered, seemingly missing the subtle exchange of tones. "We have a few appointments over there today. But I'm considering canceling them regardless of what happens here. I'd rather be closer to Mary, not farther."

"We very much hope we can accommodate your needs here, in the Cabins," Michael jumped in, anxiously. "We have contracted with a national internet and cable provider: the same one that serves Lowell, in fact. The service here is perhaps slightly lower in quality than Lowell or any other mid-sized or big city, but high-speed internet surely exists, as do reliable phone lines. I would, however, recommend that you acquire a backup generator for infrequent power outages."

They passed down a long lane of mostly-complete homes, each surprisingly different from the last and all of them something out of a catalog of modern cabin mansions. It felt like a new world to Anna, who had only ever known Maplewood houses to be small homesteads or hunting lodges. Sure, there were a few landmark homes off the main drag that looked like they were trucked in from Aspen, but there was no developed community like this.

Anna was impressed in spite of herself. She never would have predicted her hometown to become a hot spot for designer living. Yet here she was, at the end of an impressive lineup of rustic, wooden chalets, A-frames, and log cabins. It seemed as though each home site was situated on at least an acre of wooded forest, which explained why she hadn't noticed the building project on her journeys up from Phoenix. The community was very private and very beautiful.

Anna had cooled off by the time Dutch pulled the truck in front of a massive, cleared lot at the end of the lane. There were no other home sites in the general vicinity, and it appeared they had reached what was effectively a cul-de-sac.

Dutch threw the truck into park and twisted in his seat to address Kurt and Michael.

"Michael, why don't you explain to Kurt our reserved lots?"

Michael allowed a wry smile to creep up his cheeks before launching into something of a lecture on the original site plans for Maplewood Luxury Cabins. As he excitedly described the "Reserved Lots" and his own hopes for drawing in Phoenix bigwigs, the four slowly climbed out of the truck and meandered back together at the base of the treeless expanse.

Pausing for a breath, the architect looked expectantly from Kurt to Anna, then back to Kurt.

Ever the people-pleaser, Kurt smiled widely. "I'm counted as a Phoenix big-wig these days, eh?" He gently elbowed Anna, much to her irritation.

Anna stole a glance at Dutch. Thumbs hooked in his jeans pockets, he was staring directly at her, his face unreadable in the mid-morning sun.

Dutch blinked and put his hand up to shield his eyes before reigning in the conversation. "We aren't yet breaking ground on corner lots or double lots. We expect these to be custom builds. Perhaps that would be up your alley, Mr. Cutler?"

Loving the flattery, Kurt agreed that it would and allowed Dutch and Michael to walk him around the naked forest floor while Anna decided to hang back and observe.

Without Mary overhearing, she and Kurt had managed to discuss his plans more concretely. He did absolutely want to buy a home in Maplewood, and he wanted to buy one in which he'd raise a family with Mary. Anna reminded him that if he wanted an in-home office, he'd need to be in lower Maplewood, farther away from the Lodge and closer to utilities and amenities. He was hesitant and had asked her if Mary might just prefer to make a home together in the Lodge. Fortunately for her sister, Anna was there to correct him on that. She had hoped that this last-minute tour would offer a no-brainer opportunity, Kurt would sign on the dotted line, and she could stop discussing the future marriage of her sister to her boss.

But there was Dutch. Studly as ever in his butt-hugging jeans and snug flannel. Anna was distracted and interested and confused all at once. Only days ago she had contemplated joining the convent. Now here she was again, ready for action. She forced herself to stop staring and redirected her attention to her phone, which had beeped to life once they'd parked at the lot.

Are you guys coming back for lunch? Or what's the plan?

It was Mary. She had forgotten that Anna promised their parents a visit.

Kurt's dropping me off at Mom and Dad's. Gonna eat lunch there and hang out. Robbie'll bring me back tonite.

She hit send as the men started ambling back toward the truck.

Maybe Kurt can come pick me up and we can join? Other guests checked out already…I'm guessing Michael is going to come back to grab his family soon?

Anna shook her head to herself. She needed a break from both Kurt and Mary and especially from their sickeningly sweet relationship saga.

No, no. You two enjoy some private time. I'll see ya for dinner. Love ya.

Just as she slid her phone into her back pocket, the guys had returned.

Anna wasn't sure if she should glare at Dutch or smile. She did neither.

"I'm very interested," Kurt announced. "Can we talk specifics today, or are you two heading out of town soon?"

"Unfortunately, I do have to return to Mesa," Michael answered. "My daughter has a dance recital tonight."

Kurt pressed his lips together thoughtfully as Anna darted a glance toward Dutch.

If he noticed, he didn't show it. Instead, he cleared his throat.

"I can stick around."

"Terrific, should we join you in your office here, or?" Kurt trailed off.

"It's not my office, technically," Dutch chuckled. "We can certainly talk there, or if you'd prefer to grab a bite for lunch together?"

Anna could have sworn he peeked at her from the corner of his eye, if only momentarily. But, she found her footing and pursed her lips.

Kurt replied, "I can take you up to the Lodge. My girlfriend makes a mean turkey sandwich. Anna, how does that sound?"

It was Michael's turn to chime in, cutting her off. "That's a great idea! I tried to convince Dutch to check in last night..." Dutch threw Michael off with a pointed look, but Michael barreled ahead. "Dutch, this is the perfect opportunity for you to mingle with the locals. Why not stay there tonight? It'll give you plenty of time to talk shop with Mr. Cutler, and you can learn the lay of the land?"

"Good idea, Mike," Dutch returned, his face and voice flat.

"Great, it's settled then!" Kurt clapped his hands together.

As they loaded into the truck to head back to the office and the other waiting vehicles, Anna felt a pang of something she couldn't quite pin down.

Once they had made it to the office and said their farewells to Michael, Kurt began to tell Dutch to follow him, but Anna interrupted.

CHAPTER EIGHTEEN

"Actually," Anna began, "Kurt is dropping me at my folks' house."

Dutch felt her eyes on him as she said so, but he ignored it.

Kurt didn't seem to notice Anna's edge but instead cut in. "That's right. Dutch, maybe you can just meet me back up at the Lodge? Mary will be delighted to greet you. I'll give her a heads up you're on your way. I won't be five minutes behind you."

"Sounds great. See you later, Mr. Cutler," Dutch nodded his head without so much as a glance at Anna and moved to climb back into his truck.

"Call me Kurt, please," the tech boss chuckled.

Dutch paused, leaning over the bed of his truck.

"Okay, *Kurt*. And, Anna, it was nice meeting you," he smirked at the tall redhead before opening the door and pulling himself in.

Just as he pulled his seatbelt strap across his taut chest, Kurt rounded the truck and came up to his window, rapping lightly.

"Real quick, Dutch. This house-buying thing... Mary doesn't know about it. It'll be a surprise. Just tell her you're the builder on a corporate offices plaza or something, all right?"

Dutch nodded and rolled the window back up before Kurt strode back to his little car.

He took his time and let Kurt pull out ahead of him. He figured he'd allow himself the chance to take in the scenery on his way to the lodge.

As Dutch rolled down the road toward the fork, he watched Kurt's and Anna's heads bob in the black sports car ahead. He had never felt instantly attracted to a woman like that. Aside from when he met Megan, of course.

Although, Anna was definitely different than Megan. Not only her wild, red hair, either. Her creamy, flawless skin and cool green eyes didn't belong in Maplewood. He couldn't picture her delicate features withstanding the bitter-cold winters.

And that wasn't all. The way she had come on to him was unsettling. He'd grown used to bold women hitting on him, pitying his widower status, clicking their tongues over poor CaitlinJo. But Anna was different. She didn't know his story. She didn't know he had a daughter or had once had a beautiful, loving wife.

Anna's approach came from somewhere natural and raw.

And for the first time in many years, Dutch was excited about it. But he stopped himself. He wouldn't allow it. He'd decided that there would not be another Megan. His heartache was too great. He had all he needed- CaitlinJo was well-cared for thanks to his flexible schedule, his mother, and the top-of-the-line preschool she attended.

Not twenty minutes later, he saw the sign he'd been looking for.

Wood Smoke Lodge.

He knocked his blinker and turned down the tree-lined drive and up to what looked to be a ski-lodge in the pines. The parking lot was narrow, and Dutch didn't want to take up two of the tiny little tourist spots. So, instead, he pulled his truck to the side of the Lodge.

He popped the door open and climbed out of the truck, stretching his long legs as he did. He hadn't gone far, but it was even cooler here, farther up the mountain and deeper into the woods.

Just as he began to climb the steps of the front deck, the door burst open and out stepped a small-statured woman with wild, brown hair. Despite her slight build, she seemed to take up the whole doorway.

"Dutch McCree?" Her voice trilled out to him. He nodded politely and smiled.

"Yes, ma'am?"

"Mary Delaney, at your service," she called in response. "Please, please. Do come in!"

Before Dutch could introduce himself as the builder at the Cabins, Mary chattered on. He was silently glad for her rambling about the history of Wood Smoke because he had almost forgotten his cover. This gave him an opportunity to rehearse Kurt's plan.

Mary gave him a tour of the property, allowing Dutch to marvel at the vaulted, tongue-and-groove pine ceilings and imposing stone fireplace. He let his hands slide up the waxed, knotty banister as they climbed up to the guest rooms.

"Anna always bunks with me. Kurt takes the Stag Room. I'll put you in," Mary paused, leaning left to peer down the hall and giving herself a better view of the little room placards. "Bear," she finished with a knowing grin. Dutch wasn't sure what to make of the mischievous smile, but he nodded along and stepped into the room once Mary unlocked it with an old-fashioned little skeleton key.

The petite innkeeper excused herself to prepare lunch, leaving Dutch to awkwardly pace around the simple but cozy room. He suddenly felt empty-handed and self-conscious. He had worn both his clean outfits by now and all that was left in his hollow overnight duffle was the white tee shirt he'd worn to bed and yesterday's outfit. He pulled the jeans and shirt out and laid them across the bed so that they didn't wrinkle too much. They were clean enough for the morning, but he'd be sure to dash directly after breakfast.

He started to regret that he agreed to stay over another night and pulled his phone out to call home.

CaitlinJo answered his mom's cell on the first ring. "Daddy!" She shrieked into his ear before falling into a fit of giggles.

"Hey, babygirl," he cooed back, waiting for her to reel in from the sillies.

"Daddy! I'm staying with Meemaw and Bumpa tonight!"

"I know, baby. Are you having fun down there?"

"Yes!" She squealed again. Just as Dutch began to reply with an "I love you," his mom came on the line.

"We're just fine, Dutch. You enjoy the mountains. It's good for you to get away from time to time. Maybe go out on the town with that architect or something." His mom directed, not bothering to quell her bossy tone.

"I'm fine, Mom. I'll be on the road first thing tomorrow morning. Don't spoil that little girl. Okay?"

"See you tomorrow, Dutch," she clucked back.

"Love ya, Ma. Tell Cait I love her, too."

He clicked off his phone and decided to head back downstairs to see if Cutler had returned. If he was going to stick around, he'd better make a sale. After all, there was nothing else to do in this little, backwoods mountain village.

Especially if Anna wasn't going to be around.

CHAPTER NINETEEN

Kurt walked Anna up to her parents' front stoop, which irritated her. She knew him well enough to know he wasn't putting on a show for her parents. He was genuinely interested in saying hello. But, her bad mood got in the way of appreciating anything at the moment.

The little, old cabin had withstood the test of time on Maplewood Mountain. It was the exact same one that Anna's great-grandparents had built at the turn of the twentieth century. Anna's maternal ancestors had made their way up the mountain with some of the earliest groups of pioneers, which earned them a generous sect of land at the base of what was now Maplewood Proper.

As a child and teenager, Anna never appreciated the craftsmanship that went into that original family homestead. Now, she looked at it with awe. Her parents religiously maintained the woodwork, and they never failed to have the property that surrounded the immediate area of the home landscaped to perfection. Gardening had become her mother's hobby, ever since Anna's brothers, Robbie and Alan, had taken on day-to-day operations of the property. It had morphed from a modest farm and small ranch to now an apple orchard and a barn in which the brothers built a rustic, little bar and hosted town events and dances. It was at once modern and old-fashioned. The Delaneys made enough income on seasonal activities to float them for the year, and comfortably. Still, the family business was quaint.

Kurt held open the screen door as Anna ascended onto the porch and took it upon herself to open the main, wooden door before hollering, "Mom! Dad? It's me. I'm home!" She breathed in a heady potpourri bubbling on the wood-burning stove and dropped her purse on the tiny hutch next to the door before sinking into her dad's broken-in leather recliner. Kurt stood, expectant, behind the chair, his hands tucked into his jean pockets.

Anna let her eyes close for a moment, as she thought back to Dutch McCree. His name called to mind early Arizona outlaws, and she wondered where his family was from.

"Hey there, sissy," came a voice from beyond the living room. It was Robbie, stepping in from the back porch. Anna pulled herself up and a wide grin spread up her cheeks.

"Robbie Bobby!" She squealed before falling into her big brother's bear hug. He smelled like hops, and she pushed back, scrunching her nose. "New beer recipe?"

"Yep. We're working out some kinks in a new ale," he replied before striding across the living room to Kurt, who put out his hand earnestly. "Well, if it isn't the big-city computer guy," Robbie joked, pulling Kurt in for a warm hug. "I think you've got the wrong sister, here, bud," he threw a sidelong glance to Anna, who arched her eyebrow and pinned him with a pointed look.

"Just dropping Anna off before I head back up to Wood Smoke," Kurt replied, smiling.

"You staying for lunch? Mom and Dad went out to pick up KFC, Anna's favorite."

Kurt threw a curious look to Anna, who flushed and broke into a grin.

She held up her hands and shrugged.

"Hm, I never would have guessed," Kurt chuckled. "Actually, Mary has lunch planned for me. So, I'd better be going. Good to see you, Robbie. Give your parents my best."

Once Kurt had left, Robbie settled onto the couch next to Anna, where they caught up on life for the next ten minutes. Anna didn't tell Robbie about her latest Vegas trip or her decision to stop going out. He probably didn't even know she was living such a fast life to begin with.

Anna listened on as Robbie told her about how the kids were growing like weeds, and she stared into the screen on his photo, admiring sweet photos of her nieces and nephews. She promised him she'd swing by to visit sooner or later.

Finally, her parents emerged through the front door, juggling greasy paper buckets between them. Anna stood to greet them.

"Anna Banana!" Her dad called as her mom dumped the meal onto the long kitchen table and rushed to tug Anna's thin frame down into a cozy hug.

"Anna Delaney, have you been eating?" Her mother pinched the skin at her svelte waist as she clicked her tongue in disapproval. Her mom had never gotten the memo that calorie counting was commonplace in most parts of the country. Still, Anna wasn't calorie counting. She just didn't have much of an appetite lately.

"Mom, I've just been busy," Anna whined as she slumped down onto the bench that framed the kitchen table.

"Well, we're gonna have a little chat about that, young lady," Margaret chided. "Rob, is Alan coming over? The girls and kids?" She asked through swallows of sweet tea.

"Nope. Most of the kids are at sleepovers tonight, and I sort of forgot to mention that you'd be here. Well, I sort of forgot myself," Robbie admitted, sheepishly.

Anna frowned, but she understood. She'd only just mentioned to her mom the day before that she'd be in town and wanted to say hello. Still, she was a little surprised and disappointed that they hadn't thrown a party. Anna almost never took the time to hang out at the farm. Whenever she was in Maplewood, she would typically hunker down with Mary at Wood Smoke. She felt more comfortable there. At the Lodge, she wasn't under Margaret's magnifying glass or subject to her dad's awkward attempts at prying about whether she'd met anyone suitable. They were too old-fashioned for Anna.

"So, Anna Banana, are you staying the night with us? Should we set up the spare room?" her dad asked, hope filling his barrel chest.

Just as Anna was about to answer that she was considering it, her mother interrupted.

"Anna, darlin', tell us all about Kurt and Mary. We are just dying to know. Do you think he's going to propose?"

Anna's face fell, and she knew the answer to her dad's question.

Even through her disappointment, she obliged her mother and offered tidbits about Kurt and Mary. She confided that she thought they were pretty serious. Dodging her mother's nosey questions about sleeping arrangements at the Lodge, Anna asked Robbie for a tour of the property. She hadn't been out to his little Barn Bar since he'd opened it five years back.

"Sorry about Mom," Robbie muttered as they walked through the orchard together.

"It's fine," Anna replied softly through a cracking voice.

"Anna, what's wrong? You can't let her get to you like that," Robbie stopped and turned to his sister, who was now full-on crying. "Anna, you have a terrific life. You can't second guess all the great experiences you're having just because Mom is living in 1952," he pulled her into a side hug.

Anna's choking sobs slowly subsided as she began to answer him.

"It's not just Mom, Rob. I'm," she paused, sputtering out a remaining sob. "I'm *not happy*."

CHAPTER TWENTY

Dutch rubbed his eyes open and rolled across the comfortable, queen-sized bed in the Bear Room. He had decided he would skip lunch in favor of a nap, especially when Kurt and Mary started making eyes across the old farmhouse table in the dining room.

He sat at the edge of the bed as he warmed to his surroundings. The high-beam ceilings and pine walls added to the atmosphere, and Dutch made a mental note of potential upgrade ideas for the Cabins. He cocked his wrist up and noted it was just after five. He certainly hadn't meant to sleep so long. Clearly, long days on job sites and long evenings with CaitlinJo had taken their toll. The trips up to Maplewood didn't help.

He couldn't quite tell if he felt rejuvenated or even sleepier. So, he sat for a few moments more to give himself time to wake up from the post-nap fog.

Finally, he pushed off the bed and sauntered to the bathroom, where he splashed cool water on his face, admiring the claw foot tub. *Nice touch*, he thought. He ran his hand through his dark-blonde hair and went to his overnight bag where he grabbed his toothbrush. He figured he ought to look presentable for dinner. It was his final opportunity to lock Kurt into a sale.

Dutch didn't much care for trying to win the heart of a local finance mogul, but he did care enough about his business to make the effort. Michael had convinced him that they may even be able to use Kurt in future promos or something, which did little more than make Dutch cringe.

He finally felt fresh enough to leave the room and meander down the staircase. As he descended, he heard murmuring rise from the great room. The vaulted ceilings only accentuated echoes; the rugs and leather furniture offered little in the way of absorption. Before he had gotten halfway down the steps, he peeked over the railing.

Kurt was on the love seat, his back to the staircase. Dutch could see a set of legs lying across Kurt's thighs. Kurt's hands cupped the back of Mary's head and her arms were linked behind his neck.

His annoyance grew back, and Dutch wished he had just driven home. Awkwardly, he began to creep back up the stairs. Just as he turned to ascend, the front door burst open, and in stomped the tall, fire-haired beauty. Anna.

Dutch froze in place as he watched the drama unfold.

Mary flung her legs off Kurt and onto the floor, and Kurt sprang up, almost knocking Mary back across the coffee table. Mary rubbed the back of her hand over her mouth, and Kurt adjusted his waistband, nervously.

Dutch covered a small grin with his own hand and waited, enjoying the show.

"Anna!" Mary shrilled before pushing off of Kurt to round the love seat and hustle to her sister. "I didn't know if you were coming back. Is everything okay? How'd it go with Mom and Dad?"

Dutch could barely make it out, but Anna's face seemed different than that morning.

"Kurt, will you go check on dinner while we talk?" Mary directed her dark-haired boyfriend away as she pulled Anna's limp arm over to the little reception desk. Before Dutch realized he needed to go back up or make his presence known, Anna caught a glimpse of him.

They locked eyes for a moment, and Dutch began to stutter to life.

"Hi, uh, Anna, is it?" He slowly moved down a few steps, keeping his gaze steady on her. She didn't look away, and as

Dutch landed onto the modest foyer, he could tell that her face looked to be scrubbed clean. Her eyes red and watery.

Mary interjected, "Mr. McCree, hello! Hope you enjoyed your rest. Kurt's just in the kitchen if you'd like to join him there? Or maybe take a walk in the woods?" Her eyes were pleading, but Dutch didn't plan on a confrontation.

"Oh, sure. I'll make myself busy. Don't mind me, ladies," he stuffed his hands in his pockets and gave a short bow before moving past them and into the kitchen. He could feel Anna's eyes follow him, but he did everything in his power to ignore the burning sensation.

As he stepped into the kitchen, he could hear the women begin to murmur to each other in low voices, and his heart stilled for a beat. This morning, it was apparent that Anna was gorgeous. But seeing her now, different, it gave him pause. He tried to wipe her eyes off of him and cleared his throat.

Kurt turned from sipping at a crockpot.

"That smells delicious," Dutch commented. Kurt smiled at him.

"It is. Mary is a fantastic cook. This is just a simple pot roast, but my Lord," Kurt hummed. "So, Dutch?" Kurt's voice rose in question as he returned the ladle and leaned back against the counter top. "Tell me a little about yourself. Where in the valley do you live?"

As the two made small talk, Dutch couldn't help but feel distracted by the distressed Anna. What had happened at her parents' house? She was obviously crying. Was it because of his brashness towards her that morning? He hoped not. The last thing he needed was to complicate a business transaction because he treated the client's girlfriend's sister like he treated every other woman. As he thought that, Dutch's heart sank.

"Bisbee, eh?" Kurt carried on, clueless as to Dutch's sudden realization. Dutch tried to regain his footing.

"Yeah, my dad was a miner until the copper mine shut down in '85. He ended up establishing a little landscaping business right after. My mom continued to work nights as a barkeep in the Gulch," Dutch's voice faded out, and he looked over his shoulder for the girls.

"The Gulch? What's that? Bisbee's premier nightclub?" Kurt laughed.

"Brewery Gulch. It's a little avenue with bars. Historical place. Anyway," Dutch swallowed, suddenly nervous.

"I've heard of Brewery Gulch," a voice came behind him. Dutch whipped around. It was just Mary. No Anna.

"Oh yeah?" Dutch peered behind her, seeing a tall, lithe body slowly climb the stairs.

"Hey, when you're in the Arizona tourism biz, you have to know your stuff. Anyway, Bisbee is a southwest legend. What, with all the ghosts and hippies, all that?" Mary smiled warmly to Dutch as she slid around him and backed into Kurt, who wrapped her in his arms. Dutch turned the left side of his mouth up, examining the lovebirds. Even he and Megan hadn't been that smitten.

"That's right. Ghosts and hippies. And McCree outcasts."

"Outcasts?" Kurt asked, pointedly.

"Once I graduated from high school, I wanted out. I didn't see a future for any of us in Bisbee. I mean, don't get me wrong. I love the place. And, I really miss living in a small, rural town. But my wife," Dutch broke off, suddenly, before restarting. "I didn't want to worry about being out on my rear because of a dying industry. So I took up a trade and moved us out of there."

"Does your wife miss it? Bisbee, that is?" Mary asked.

Dutch glanced to the left and shifted his weight.

"She passed," he replied, looking down at his work boots. Just as Mary began to offer her sympathy, a voice came up from behind Dutch.

"Who passed?"

Dutch turned around to see Anna standing in the kitchen doorway, her hair in wild tangles around her clean face. She had changed into hip-hugging jeans and a Southwestern University sweatshirt.

Dutch felt his jaw slack, and before he could answer, Mary stepped in.

"Dutch's wife," she answered for him and crossed to him, patting his arm as if she were a little, old grandmother. Dutch smiled down at her then glanced up to Anna.

Her face didn't change, but she took her hands out from her sweatshirt pocket and brushed a fallen strand from her eyes.

"Sorry," Anna added, looking at Mary.

"That's really awful, Dutch. I'm sorry, too." Kurt met Dutch's gaze and nodded seriously.

"It's been two years. I've accepted it. I'm not much for talking it to death, so to speak," Dutch couldn't help but chuckle at the dark, unintentional pun. It lightened the mood enough to redirect everyone's attention off of him, thankfully.

Anna stepped into the kitchen fully and leaned herself against the sink. "So, what's for dinner? I'm starving."

CHAPTER TWENTY-ONE

Anna had ended up skipping lunch at her parents' house and took a long walk with Robbie instead. She brought him up to speed on her Vegas trip after all, and he let her sort of review the last several years of her life, judgment-free. She loved her brother for that. He was always happy to listen and only chimed in with uplifting comments or suggestions. Her sisters would do the same, but they all seemed so busy with their own drama.

When Robbie asked her why she thought she even wanted a change, the answer surfaced slowly. By the time they had finished nearly two miles of looping around the farm, Robbie had drawn it out of her. But it was a truth her whole family had already known.

***

Anna had fallen hard and fast for Danny Flanagan. The whole town knew they'd end up a high school-sweethearts success story. Anna had counted on it. She saw herself becoming the picture-perfect Maplewood wife and mother, living near her parents and having dinner ready for Danny when he got home from firefighting or policing or some other glamorous, mountain-town career.

Two months before graduation, she woke up in the middle of the night with a pain like she had never known. She tried to make her way to the bathroom but couldn't and instead crouched at her bedside, doubled-over from the deep, sudden ache. There was a heaviness in her lower abdomen, and with every moment a new lightning bolt of pain would rock her body. After what felt like an hour of the painful onslaught, she cried out to Bo, who was asleep in their shared room.

Anna woke up the next morning in a hospital bed in Lowell.

She had barely made it, the doctors chided.

She asked her mother, who was fretting at her bedside, what had happened. Her mother explained in hushed tones that Anna had been pregnant. Two months along. It was an ectopic pregnancy, and it burst. Anna nearly bled to death. In order to save her life, the doctors had to perform immediate surgery.

Anna sobbed cold, jerking sobs. Her mother alternated between comforting her and questioning her. How could this happen? Was it Danny? Had Anna known all along?

Anna had no answers for her mother. Only one more question.

Where was Danny?

She got her answer once she returned to school the following week.

He was in the arms of another girl.

By the time Anna learned that her chances of having future children were halved, at best, she no longer cared.

***

Robbie hugged her hard. His compassion for their shared memory of what Anna had been through broke her down even further. Her face crumpled and she, for the first time in a long time, cried for her mom.

When Robbie guided a weeping Anna back into the little log cabin, Margaret Delaney practically threw her crispy drumstick across the room before dashing to the door to take Anna in her arms. It was an uncommon display for the matriarch.

They talked the rest of the afternoon. Margaret apologized and joined Anna in crying. Richard squeezed down onto the sofa between the mother and daughter, resuming his role of buffer from the trying days when Anna was a teenager.

They talked about everything from Anna's pregnancy to her disappearance into college and then a career all the way through to her current, wild lifestyle.

As they hashed it out, it occurred to Anna that she had wanted to be scolded all those years. Not guilted. Not shamed. She wanted to be outright scolded. She wanted them to tell her she messed up. But, she also wanted them to tell her that none of it was her fault and that someone would fix it for her.

They never did.

***

Still hurt, Anna said her farewells to her parents. Despite lingering hard feelings on Anna's end, their hugs felt good.

Robbie agreed to drive Anna up to Wood Smoke Lodge and drop her off. Once they arrived, Anna invited Robbie in to say hi to Mary and Kurt, but he passed on the offer. Anna forgot that Mary had resumed joining the family for Sunday dinners again. The recollection made Anna wince a little. She gave Robbie another big hug and scooted into the Lodge, where she had yet another breakdown to Mary and almost in front of the obnoxiously attractive contractor. Fortunately, he had enough sense to excuse himself and let her talk to her sister privately.

Mary took a hard line with Anna, however. She reminded her older sister that Anna had the power to make decisions that made her happy. She didn't think Anna should hold it against their parents that they didn't tell Anna what she wanted to hear.

Mary reassured Anna that the pregnancy was not a mistake and that it was a very traumatic and difficult experience, to which Anna started crying all over again.

After her stay in the hospital, she thought she'd fall back into Danny's loving arms and they would make it work. Still get married. Maybe still have their own children or, at least, adopt eventually. She had thought it all through in the short time she was stuck at home healing.

But when Danny moved on without a second thought-without even knowing Anna was pregnant with *his* child, she shut down. Suddenly, Anna's future had changed. There was no happily-ever-after. She'd have to make her own way in the world without her high school sweetheart.

So, she got herself into Southwestern and worked her butt off to become a whole other person. A smart woman who could support herself. Who didn't need a boyfriend or a husband. Who didn't care about having children. Maybe, she didn't even want them anyway.

Once she had thrown herself into her schooling and then her career, she started to pick away at the hurt Danny had left in her heart. Every boy she had met from then on became a version of Danny. Anna used and abused them all. And she never once regretted it.

And then she started at FantasyCoin and began to feel a stability she hadn't known since she lived at home. Kurt's company had become her little family, even if they didn't realize it. The team members were her little siblings. Kurt, well, she didn't know where he fit in the family. But, once he set his sights on Mary, Anna felt a betrayal almost as deep as Danny's. Working there for only a year made it even worse. She saw FantasyCoin as the beginning of something.

Maybe, it was the end.

CHAPTER TWENTY-TWO

M ary, God bless her, was able to lift the mood.
"Mama's Mountain Pot Roast!" She answered brightly.
Dutch lifted an eyebrow.

"Mama's?" he asked, looking between the sisters and Kurt.

"Our mama's," Anna replied, a hint of amusement in her voice. "Everything Mary makes is a rip off of a Margaret Delaney recipe. When Mary first opened the Lodge, she tried to recreate our mom's mac-and-cheese, but it was sort of a failure. So, Alan called it Mama's Mountain Mac, sort of as a joke. It stuck." She smirked at him, and there was a glint of *something* in her eye.

"Sounds...questionable, then," he shot back, half-smiling. Mary burst out laughing, and Kurt followed. Anna even smiled.

"It's not, I assure you," Kurt chimed in. "Mary has proven herself to be an exceptional cook and baker. Best in Maplewood, I'd say," Kurt finished.

"Kurt, you haven't been around Maplewood long enough to know that," Anna scoffed. "Technically, Leslie Zick is the best cook and baker in town. Her cinnamon rolls are so delicious that the local paper officially named them the hottest buns on the mountain."

"Now *that* I *absolutely dis*agree with," Kurt playfully slapped Mary's behind, horrifying Anna and throwing Dutch deeper into an unprecedented fit of laughter. Kurt and Mary joined him, but Anna held back. He didn't care. He laughed good and hard for a full minute.

Dutch couldn't remember the last time he'd cracked up with other adults. His playful interactions had been limited to Barbie picnics and tea parties. CaitlinJo flashed through his mind, and his laughter fell off.

He missed her.

The others began to converge on the crockpot as Mary served hearty helpings onto quaint, porcelain dishes. Kurt and Anna carried their plates and glasses of water into the adjoining dining room, and Dutch waited for Mary to serve him.

"Thank you, ma'am," he took the plate from her hands and nodded.

"You're welcome, Cowboy," she giggled back. Dutch paused before going into the dining room.

"Happen to have any beer? Or whiskey? I'm not particular," he asked, earnestly.

Mary's lips fell into a line, but it was Anna's voice behind him that responded.

"Mary doesn't keep alcohol here, but I know of a little watering hole nearby if you're looking for a nightcap?" Dutch turned to see her in the doorway, a hand on one hip, the other pushing against the doorframe at eye level.

Dutch took note of her unreadable expression, her eyes boring a hole into his head. He glanced back at Mary, who was staring at her sister, her mouth slightly open.

"Um," Dutch scratched his head with his free hand. Anna lifted a perfectly arched eyebrow. He dropped his hand. "Sure?"

***

Dinner was awkward. Kurt tried to make conversation about the Cabins, and Dutch was happy to oblige him, but Mary and Anna barely spoke a word to each other. Until Mary got up to clear the dishes.

"Anna, a word?" She demanded, her voice firm. She had done a 180 from the joyful, people-pleaser she'd seemed to be. And Anna, for her part, seemed to have moved past whatever had upset her. Dutch watched, confused, as the two women disappeared into the kitchen.

"Am I, um, missing something?" he finally asked Kurt. Dutch wasn't one to intervene in people's personal lives, but he wasn't about to head to a bar with his client's business partner if there was danger ahead.

"Sister stuff, I guess," Kurt replied, wiping his mouth with a paper napkin. "Anna and Mary haven't spent much time together lately. In fact, I don't think they've seen each other since Christmas," Kurt thought for a moment before smiling at Dutch. "That's when I met Mary, actually," he continued.

Dutch nodded along, listening to how Kurt and Mary hit it off. Love-at-first-sight-type thing. He could see Kurt's attraction to Mary. Both she and Anna definitely had *something*. Mary was a little too bubbly and sweet for his tastes, though. Not that he had a taste for any woman, anymore. Or at least, not for anything serious.

He shook off his uneasy feeling and listened as Kurt wrap up the tale of a little holiday-romance-turned-serious. Dutch knew very well what it was like to be in a serious relationship. Equal parts exciting and stressful. But Kurt didn't seem too stressed. Especially for a businessman and entrepreneur of his league. In fact, he seemed head-over-heels.

Anna swept back into the dining room.

"I'll be ready in five," she barked at the two men. Dutch blinked in return, and Anna strode purposefully out and up the staircase. Mary walked into the dining room after her, wiping her hands on a green apron. She kept her eyes on her sister as she ascended the pine stairs.

"Everything okay?" Kurt finally seemed to clue into the drama.

"She's dead-set on going out tonight, I guess," Mary sighed back at him and then looked meaningfully at Dutch. "Can you keep a close eye on her?"

Dutch frowned back. "You two aren't joining us?" He leaned back a little, anxiety creeping in.

Mary cut in before Kurt had a chance to answer. "No. Kurt and I don't drink. It'll just be the two of you."

CHAPTER TWENTY-THREE

Anna was done dealing with her emotions. She needed an outlet, and Dutch McCree would have to do. She swiped on several coats of Blackest Black mascara and puffed a bit of rouge onto her already-pronounced cheekbones. She then rummaged around in Mary's pathetic vanity until she found a fifteen-year-old bottle of *Body by Victoria* rolling along the back of a bottom drawer. She splashed some on and then darted into the bathroom where she scrubbed her teeth ruthlessly with Mary's toothbrush. Finally, she smudged gloss onto her lips, before smacking them dramatically and pouting at her reflection.

She wasn't meant to be a Mary.

She left Mary's room with nothing but a credit card and her cell phone and trotted down the stairs and into the foyer.

"Ready!" She called to no one in particular.

Anna stood at the reception desk and scrolled mindlessly through her phone, ignoring texts from Jenna and Amber and Jessica. Passing her eyes across Roberta's fifth attempt at calling. Finally, Anna navigated back to her messages to see the follow-up text Bo had sent.

Dannielle fired me, so... I'm free if you wanna do a Vegas Round 2 ;)

Ugh, Anna grunted. Bo had been fired from every writing gig and every editing job she had ever (somehow) managed to land. Anna hesitated before tapping out a quick reply.

Sorry Sis, but- again? She reread it before hitting send. Just as she was about to delete the message and offer kind, if disingenuous, words instead, Mary's voice interrupted her.

"Hey." The tension was palpable. Anna looked up and over her shoulder as Mary carefully treaded into the foyer.

"Hi," Anna huffed and pocketed her phone in the sweatshirt. She hadn't bothered to change. She didn't bring anything sexy, anyway. Just her weekend comfy clothes. Anna looked past Mary as if she was impatient for Dutch to whisk her off. Which, frankly, she was.

"Maybe you should just stay in tonight, Ann," Mary suggested delicately. "We could play cards or Monopoly?"

Anna smirked. "Sounds fun, but I need to blow off steam. You're welcome to join me." She finally met Mary's gaze.

Anna grew tired of Mary's squeaky-clean persona. Mary had never made a misstep in her life. She was almost as perfect as Erica, who married right away and steadily popped out tow-headed angels over the last several years. Sure, it took Mary a while longer to find her Prince Charming, but she was certainly better loved by Margaret and Richard than either Anna or Roberta.

Anna and Bo had committed to never let it bother them that they had become the black sheep of the family. But it did bother Anna. She had not originally set out for a life like she came to have. Fortunately, she ended up falling in love with her career. And the travel! She had traveled far and wide and experienced nearly everything life had to offer.

Of course, Anna had never found another true love. Not after Danny. Or the "accident," as it had become known as. But she had experienced it once, and that was more than enough for her. Sometimes, she did feel a little unmoored and rootless. But, she had experienced everything in life that she had wanted to. Almost.

Once she returned to Maplewood and was forced to be party to Kurt and Mary's sickeningly sweet romance, it began to feel like life was crashing down around her. Vegas maybe wasn't rock bottom, after all.

"I'm not judging you, Anna. But, we just talked about this last night. Have you forgotten?" Mary asked. She looked like she genuinely thought Anna had forgotten about their long talk in bed. The one in which Anna had convinced Mary that she was giving up booze and boys. She was refocusing, especially now that she was about to be co-president with Kurt. Mary was excited for her. She thought that Anna would find renewed energy and happiness, and Anna agreed.

But it sounded lame. And boring.

At least she had a solid job. Why couldn't that be enough for Anna?

Before she had a chance to respond to Mary, Dutch emerged on the staircase. He'd rolled his sleeves and pulled on a black baseball cap. His five o'clock shadow seemed to have darkened above his sharp jawline, and his fingers were crammed tightly into his front jeans pockets as he trotted smoothly down the steps.

Anna swallowed hard.

"I'll drive," she demanded, putting her hand out for his keys. She felt him study her freshly made-up face, but he didn't flinch.

"Nope," he answered, his voice flat.

"But you don't know your way around. It'll be easier; here, just let me." Anna stepped away from Mary and toward Dutch, who had paused at the base of the staircase.

"I have a good sense of direction. You can tell me where to go. But, I'm driving. Or, maybe you can take Mary's jeep," he shrugged and actually began to turn up the stairs.

Anna was floored. She glanced back at Mary, who was doing little to hide a little smile. Kurt had walked in from the kitchen, drying his hands on a towel. Had he been helping her do the dishes? Ugh.

"Fine," she answered loudly and looked back up to Dutch who had ascended a few steps.

He turned and grinned. "Great. Let's go, girl."

CHAPTER TWENTY-FOUR

Dutch was surprised at how Anna acted in front of Kurt, her boss. If he didn't know better, he'd consider her spoiled. But he had gotten the clear picture that the Delaney sisters were raised to be hard-working, humble women.

Still, Anna just didn't fit the mold. She seemed a little unpredictable. Nothing like Megan was. Megan, the even-keeled, stable homemaker who had little in the way of professional or personal ambitions. Megan was just happy to watch reality T.V. and plop in microwavable dinners for the three of them. Sometimes she'd cook up hot dogs or burgers.

Once they were in the car, Anna had cooled off a bit. Instead of indulging him in small talk, she played navigator. Right out of the Lodge driveway, five minutes up the mountain, left into the muddy lot just off the main drag.

The Last Chance Saloon.

The name of the place seemed cheesy, like it was trying too hard. But, Anna swore it was a Maplewood original. At least, the name was. The real original drinking hole burned down in the early 1900s, but descendants of the founders resurrected the little dive bar at the start of Maplewood's heyday in the '70s.

Dutch threw the truck into park and hopped out to head around the front and open Anna's door for her. By the time he got there, his boots caked in the pale mud that follows winter, she was already crossing the tiny parking lot and mounting the modest front walk of the bar.

Dutch frowned at the fiery red hair that pooled out and around Anna's college sweatshirt.

He strode over to catch the door for her on the way in, his long legs closing in on her just before she got there. She pulled her hood back and shook the early March chill. Dutch stomped his boots before stepping in behind her.

Dimly lit with country music blaring from a dark corner, the place looked every bit its name. Dutch made out a short bar and five or six high tops peppered at the edges of a modest, vinyl dance floor. There was one lone couple slowly swaying to the tune of "The Chair," while three other couples and one small group watched on from their seats.

Dutch couldn't decide if he liked the joint. It was nothing like the club he'd once gone to with Megan when they first moved to the big city. Colorful and strange with scores of twenty-somethings bumping along to obnoxious techno music, he felt uncomfortable there.

On the other hand, it wasn't much like any of the bars on Bisbee's Brewery Gulch, either. Small and dark, yes. But those establishments glowed with people from all walks of life and were filled with strange smells and the music of local artists.

Here, he seemed to have fallen back in time several decades. He half-expected Dolly Parton or even John Wayne to amble up to the bar and order a round for everyone.

Anna might have read his mind. She pointed to the lone high-top that was unoccupied and called back to him that she'd be right back. Moments later, the man singing paused his set and made an announcement.

"One of the Delaney sisters is here tonight, y'all," he started, grinning up at Anna, who was facing the barkeep. "This round's on her, ladies and gentlemen." As he finished his announcement, the small crowd clapped and whistled loudly.

Anna turned back around, a shot glass in each hand, and nodded briefly at the appreciative patrons.

The band switched gears to a Toby Keith number just as Anna climbed onto her chair and slid a tequila across to Dutch. He winced.

"That was generous," he commented, his arms crossed and elbows propped on the waxed oak top.

"Dutch McCree," she said, taking the whole of the glass in one swallow, "I'm celebrating."

"Celebrating what, exactly?"

"My promotion. No one has celebrated me. No office party. No dinners with friends. No mention from my folks. My sisters barely complimented me. So, you're celebrating with me. My meteoric rise to fame as a cryptocurrency and app development female prodigy. No one else like me," she boasted, slapping her hands down on the table. "Drink up, Dutch," she demanded.

Dutch studied the amber liquid. "This isn't exactly what I had in mind, Miss Delaney." He lifted his eyes to hers. His face expressionless.

"Either you drink that or dance with me." She copied him, crossing her arms and propping her elbows.

Dutch had rarely been in this position: a woman bossing him around left and right. He couldn't quite tell if he liked it.

He kind of did. But he couldn't expose himself.

"I don't negotiate with terrorists, Miss," he answered, looking off to the dance floor to see that two other couples had joined the original. They were two-stepping across the faux wooden panels, the women's hair flying back, the men breaking in their stiff Wranglers.

"Okay, fine. But call me Anna," she shot back and grabbed his glass, downing it instantly.

"Whoa, slow down, there girl." Dutch stared at her, his mouth set. Behind her eyes, he saw something flash. It looked like the memory of a distant dream. Strange but familiar. He sighed. "Okay, I'll grab my own drink, and then we can talk about what happens next." He pushed off the stool and strode over to the bar. He felt her eyes on him, but he didn't look back.

"Whiskey, straight up," he ordered. The drink splashed across to him. He threw down a ten and returned to the table, where he slowly nursed the bitter drink.

"Tell me about yourself, Dutch." If she was put off by him, it certainly didn't show.

"Not much to tell," he said as he kept his eyes on the dancing lovers.

"Oh, bull. Everyone's got a story. Even the perfect Delaney sisters have skeletons in their closets," she smirked.

"Everyone may have a story, but stories don't always mean skeletons." Dutch didn't want to engage in small-town gossip, and he definitely didn't want to be fodder for it.

"Okay, then tell me about your happy, little life as an impeccable, Scottsdale contractor, then. Why the Maplewood project?" She dug.

"Nothin' much exciting about it. Just a business opportunity was all." Dutch took a deeper sip.

"Phoenix keeps growing. Why not keep your work close to home?" Dutch knew he had nothing to hide. But she was making him feel like he did. He wasn't about to tolerate an inquisition. Brooks and Dunn came on next. One of Dutch's favorite.

"Wanna dance?" He asked, avoiding eye contact.

"Are you kidding?" She pushed an errant strand from her eyes and stood in front of the table, a devil's grin spreading across her face as she tucked her chin down and stared at him.

He grabbed her fragile hand and led her to the floor where he pulled her in for a slow two-step.

This woman was driving Dutch McCree crazy.

CHAPTER TWENTY-FIVE

Dutch knew his way around a country bar, Anna realized quickly. He refused to let her be in control, but that only excited her more. She found that it was nice to let someone else take the reins.

He whirled to and fro, pressing her body into his as their rhythm melted with the song. Anna was floating. And it had little to do with the two tequilas.

Buying the round for the bar felt good. Old-timey and modern- a woman tech president covering tequila shots for Maplewood locals. Anna got a kick out of it.

When Dutch continued to shut her down, she decided she simply wasn't going to stand for it. And now she was almost drunk.

As they rocked and waltzed across the scuffed floor, she closed her eyes and let go of the last few months.

The Wood Smoke Lodge Christmas Retreat fiasco. Humiliating. She let it go.

The Vegas trip meant to cheer her up. Stupid and lame. She let it go.

The personal pact to quit booze and boys. Obviously, she was letting that go.

Playing witness to Mary and Kurt's blossoming, budding, belching romance. Fine, whatever. She let it go.

Talking and crying it out with her brother and folks. That, she could not let go.

She clung to their conversation. To her mother's apology for passing judgment. Her father's apology for looking the other way. It meant the world. But why couldn't they tell her it wasn't her fault?

She could not let it go.

The second song had ended and Dutch dipped her backward, briefly. Her eyes shot open and connected with Dutch's.

She needed one more drink.

"Be right back," she purred as she untangled her hand from his. But he grabbed her wrist.

"My turn, Anna." She watched as he made his way to the bar and ordered for them. They returned to the table at the same time. Anna, reapplying lip gloss, Dutch setting down a second whiskey and a light beer. He pushed the beer to her.

"Really?" Anna scoffed.

"You've had two shots. Time to cool it. If you'd rather have a water?" He began.

She grabbed up the long neck and took a swig. "This IS water," she chortled back and wiped her mouth with the back of her hand.

"Very ladylike," Dutch jabbed. Anna glared at him. He held her gaze before holding the tiny glass up to his mouth. He threw it back in one motion then wiped his mouth with the back of his hand.

"Let's dance," he demanded. Anna felt her heart tighten in her chest, and short breaths began to collect in her throat. Instead of answering, she let him grab her hand again.

The other couples were crowding the floor. Anna began to realize that the place was warming up. There was now a healthy mix of locals and even a couple tourists, perhaps. A few younger couples were bobbing at the bar, too.

As Dutch twirled her around the floor, she began to feel hot. But she wasn't wearing a tee-shirt underneath her sweatshirt. She felt dizzy and buzzed, and she didn't want the night to end.

She pulled herself up, closer to Dutch's face. She leaned into him and raised her voice.

"Can we go outside for a minute?" She pushed back to catch his expression. Something dark passed in his eyes, and he nodded his head almost gravely.

She led the way out to the smokers' patio. Anna pulled at her sweatshirt, fanning herself with it as she stepped into the brisk air. Just as he stepped out behind her, Dutch grabbed Anna's elbow and whirled her around.

She frowned up at him, and before she had a chance to ask what he was doing, he grabbed the back of her head and pressed his mouth down onto hers.

She didn't hesitate. Anna kissed Dutch McCree like she had never kissed a man. Like she had never even kissed Danny.

He dropped his hands to the small of her back, and she reached her arms up and laced her fingers behind his neck, running her nails up under the brim of his baseball cap and into his cropped, blonde hair.

His kiss contradicted itself. Rough, but tender. Lasting, but brief.

He pulled his face away, his eyes down on the ground while his hands were still locked around her.

Anna felt like she couldn't catch her breath. She searched his face until he finally lifted his gaze.

He released her and stepped back, rubbing at his five o'clock shadow. Anna bit down on her lip and glanced around them for witnesses. When she confirmed they were still alone she took a step toward him, closing the gap. She grabbed his rough hands and pulled herself back into him.

They kissed again before he gently let go.

"Let's head back in. It's probably getting late," he suggested.

Anna sighed but agreed. They reentered to the twang of Willie Nelson. Anna decided against finishing the half-full beer and instead opted for a glass of water. Dutch joined her, and they sat in silence together.

After several minutes of contemplation, Anna made the next move.

"Should we head back? I'm a little sleepy," she stretched back, yawning. Her system hadn't completely dissolved the earlier drinks, but she was feeling a mix of exhaustion and elation. Exhaustion over an emotional day. An emotional decade, even. Elation over Dutch.

She surely hadn't expected to meet a stud that weekend. And even so, she had sworn off hooking up. Anyways, Dutch's reaction toward her advances at the Cabins threw her for a loop. No man had ever thwarted a come-on from Anna Delaney.

But then, here he was, obviously into her.

They locked eyes and Dutch replied, "Good idea. I have to leave early in the morning."

Anna couldn't read his tone or his words. But she was clinging to some degree of hope. They left, Dutch holding the bar door and the car door for her. She took an extra moment to climb up into the king cab, her sweatshirt lifting just above her waist as she did.

Once they were both settled in the cab, he turned the heat up. Anna peeked at Dutch out of the corner of her eye. He turned his focus to starting the car as if it was the most important and serious task of his life. She couldn't help but giggle.

"What?" he asked, letting a grin creep into his wide mouth.

"I don't know," she answered, moving her attention back to the road, now feeling more serious herself. "Oh, you made the wrong turn," she pointed behind them, whipping her head around.

"I know," he answered, his mouth set in a line.

Anna sucked in a breath and dormant butterflies filled her insides. She glanced around at the dark world outside of the truck. Maplewood was such a quiet, peaceful place. Almost spooky, at times. But she wasn't scared.

She was excited. A different excited than when she went to Vegas or Phoenix clubs. Even different than when good news hit FantasyCoin offices. It felt fresh.

"Where are we going?" she finally asked, watching Dutch for some indication of his mood.

"Just the long way," he replied. "I don't want to take you home only for you to stumble through the door and further upset your sister.

Anna considered his response.

"Have you ever been up to the ski slopes here? I guess you haven't. They are beautiful at night. The lifts are open until, like, ten p.m. or something. The lights on the snow... it's beautiful," she finished at last. She couldn't remember the last time she had called anything beautiful.

"How far is it?" he asked, squinting at the road ahead. It was a fair question. In the dark, you couldn't see the peaks unless you were right there.

"About ten miles, straight up," Anna pointed ahead.

Dutch cocked his head to the left and adjusted his hands on the wheel.

"Let's do it."

CHAPTER TWENTY-SIX

Dutch sneaked a glance at Anna once they were about two miles from the slopes. She had fallen quiet just after he agreed to go up. It was past nine, but they'd get there in time to catch the lights on the snow, as she said. He couldn't imagine that it would be anything special.

Anyway, Dutch didn't care about the ski slopes. He just didn't want the night to end. Any excuse to avoid creeping shamefully into the Lodge sounded good to him. But, that wasn't the only reason.

He'd never spent time with a woman like Anna. Her beauty was one thing. But her wildness was quite another. Megan had been his one-and-only true love. Even in high school he never dated. After Megan passed, he'd received countless offers of set-ups, blind dates, online dating profile ideas, and more- all from his buddies and their wives. His parents weren't shy about their druthers, either.

Dutch was a fool to give up on life at such a young age, his dad reasoned. *There'd be scores of wonderful young ladies who would jump at the chance to fill Megan's shoes*, his mom argued.

He hated hearing any of it. It wasn't that Megan was irreplaceable. But to talk like someone could just step into her place felt morbid and disrespectful. She was CaitlinJo's mother. She was a fine mother. And even if Dutch *had* met some perfect woman, no one could fill the shoes of his daughter's own, natural mother. Not possible.

Which was exactly why Dutch decided there was no real point in dating. Besides, the types of women who were showing interest did not interest *him*. He loved that Megan had stayed home with CaitlinJo. He thought it was perfect. But in his new, post-Megan world, he couldn't see a reason to date a stay-at-home mom. If there was a single one, well, that just didn't add up, anyway. He was ready for the next phase. Focusing on CaitlinJo's schooling and his own business's continued success.

The mothers at the preschool and the single women at church- not a one had struck his fancy. He only imagined their pastimes- the mothers focused on their own children (hey! No judgment there!). And the single women... well, the single women seemed to have no focus to speak of. What were they doing going after a widower with a little girl anyway?

Then today happened.

First at the office, where Anna, stunning and tall and svelte, came on strong. Dutch had no choice but to take the upper hand and shut her down on the spot. But, he didn't want to. He *had* to. Professionally, he couldn't open himself up to awkwardness. Personally, he made a deal with himself.

Then Anna returned to the Lodge. He hadn't expected that. She'd looked different. Deflated. Like someone knocked the wild out of her. And he felt a sadness and a curiosity he couldn't explain.

He didn't want to go to the bar with her, but, again, he felt he had no choice. He thought for sure Kurt would join them. When Kurt and Mary bowed out, Dutch was stuck.

Dutch McCree hated being backed into a corner. He liked control. He liked to call the shots. And he lost. He had to go.

Once he was in that little dive with its 1970s paneling offset by sturdy oak and juniper beams... that little dive with the Wrangler-wearing, hat-tipping, boot-stomping cowboys and the feather-haired, rhinestone-bloused ladies... he felt...

Home.

Maybe even for the first time in his life, if he was being honest.

Sure, he loved Bisbee. And he longed to return there, if even just for a one-night stay. He loved the interesting people.

He loved the authentic Mexican food. He especially loved the history, including his family's own history there.

But he just hadn't fit in. He wanted to see the world, just a little more of it. To know if there was somewhere he could fit in.

Scottsdale ended up being a bust, too. Sure, it offered anything a guy or gal could want. It was the perfect place for CaitlinJo to grow up. That was of the utmost importance.

But Dutch still didn't belong. Fortunately, the crazy success of McCree Construction and Outfitters solidified their place in the posh suburb. It was working. For the time being.

"Turn right here," Anna interrupted the quietness inside the truck. He did as she said. The landscape had suddenly changed. Gone was the thawing, soggy town as the truck climbed over icy patches and into a snow-crusted parking lot.

"I can't believe there's so much snow up here," Dutch commented. Sure, March was typically chilly, but coming from a place like Phoenix, one was rarely reminded that snow ever even existed.

"Some years, Maplewood doesn't even see spring. It goes from fall to winter to late June," Anna laughed. He liked seeing her lighten up.

"Sounds like the groundhog dictates the weather here." Dutch cringed at his lame joke, but Anna cracked up. His face flushed a little, and he cranked the shifter into park.

"I have a good feeling, though," Anna turned and looked at him, her eyes bright against the parking lot lights. "I think Maplewood is on the brink of its best spring yet."

Dutch smiled back at her before climbing out of the truck. He hesitated in deciding if he should even go over to open her door this time, but as he rounded the hood of the truck, he saw her sitting in there, awaiting him. He beamed a little.

As he pulled open her door, he asked, "Change your mind about the little self-sufficient-independent-woman act?" As soon as the words slipped out of his mouth he wished he could shove them back in.

But she didn't seem bothered. Instead, she chuckled and took his outstretched hand. "Something like that," she uttered before slipping down onto the salt-covered asphalt.

He wanted to know more.

"Are you some sort of new-age... ah," he paused, unable to find the perfect word. But she jumped in, saving him.

"Are *you* some sort of old-timer?" She looped her arm through his, her sweatshirt bunching at his elbow. She wasn't much shorter than he, which was impressive since he stood at nearly six foot four.

He walked her slowly through the lot and up toward the glowing snow. She was right. Even from behind the ski lodge and adjoining buildings he could tell it was a neat thing to see.

He answered, "What's that supposed to mean?"

"New-age? Who says that? Especially at, what, you can't be much older than me. And what are you getting at, anyway? Am I a man-hating hippy? Is that your angle?" She thrust her elbow into his ribs.

"Ow," he replied, half-heartedly. She giggled, and Dutch's blood seemed to grow hot despite their surroundings. "I'm 34, for your information. And, I guess that is exactly what I was asking," he admitted.

"I'm not a man-hater or a hippy. I just like to do things my way. That's all." She seemed to clam up, and he let her. They continued silently to the lodge before she directed them. Once they climbed the steps up to the back of the lodge, Anna pointed. "They have some picnic tables and chairs at the base of the bunny slope. Let's sit over there."

Poorly dressed for the conditions, the two shivered their way between the ski lodge and what looked like the rentals building, and once they'd made it through, the view really was spectacular.

Massive, football-stadium-style lights shone down on two long ski runs that disappeared up into the heavens. The snow wasn't fresh powder, but its icy patches shone brilliantly, adding to the surprising beauty.

Anna perched on one side of the table, the side facing the slopes. A shiver wracked her body, and she huddled farther into her sweatshirt. Dutch squeezed next to her, his hip on hers.

Dutch commented first. "This really is something. In Phoenix, March looks likes spring training, art festivals, and NASCAR weekends."

Anna snorted. "I know, believe me. When I was growing up here, I was so fed up with the snow come March. Like, it should feel like butterflies and warm grass already."

"Does it still bother you?" Dutch kept his eyes on the few skiers and snowboarders who slid and cut their way down the hard, compact snow.

"Honestly? Not at all. I miss it. I miss the cold weather. Why can't Phoenix have even a hint of seasons? It's just summer, summer, summer, one day of fall, summer." Now it was Dutch's turn to laugh.

"I get it. Bisbee didn't have much in the way of seasons, but it had more than the concrete jungle does. Still, it's a nice place to…" he stopped himself before he finished the sentence.

"Why'd you leave Bisbee?" Dutch felt Anna tilt her head, trying to earn his eye contact. He blinked before letting himself look at her. Her smoky eyes in dramatic contrast to the clean snow. Her red hair tucked back in the hood of her sweatshirt, exposing a long, delicate neck.

"Opportunity. Had the chance to really make something of my construction company, and I took it."

"Does your family still live there?" she pried.

Dutch hesitated thoughtfully before finally replying, "No, they're in Phoenix now, too. How about you? Do you see yourself coming back to Maplewood?" He had to change the conversation. He didn't find it the right time to talk about his circumstances.

"Oh, Lord, no." It was Anna's turn to look away. She seemed to pretend to study the slopes.

"Why not? Seems like a nice little place." He thought he knew the answer though. Maplewood probably didn't offer much in the way of a dating life. Maybe she was looking for that special guy. Dutch felt his heart skip, but he quelled it. He wasn't that special guy. Not interested. He cleared his throat as she began to answer.

"Left for college, got my degree, found a job in the tech sector, bumped around 'til I met Kurt and joined the FantasyCoin team. Never looked back. Simple as that." She returned her focus to him. If he didn't know better, he thought there was a dare in her gaze.

"Sounds pretty simple," he answered, offering a thin smile.

"Yep. I'm not Mary. Or Erica. Or even Bo, thank God," Anna laughed.

"Are they your other sisters?"

"Yep. Bo is the oldest girl, just a year younger than Alan. Roberta was her given name. We all call her Bo, ever since our little brother, Robbie, was born and Roberta refused to go by Roberta anymore. She's a wildcard. She's living in Tucson, writing. Some days, at least."

Dutch nodded, listening intently. He was fascinated by big families. He had always wanted one. He regretted being an only child, and the thing he regretted almost as much as Megan's death was that CaitlinJo had no siblings. Such a small family. A loving family, but a small one. He longed for big family gatherings with arguments and obnoxious laughter and kids tripping over the rug and punch getting spilled on his mother's white carpet.

"Then Erica. She's little miss perfect. Perfect children. Perfect baby bump. Perfect husband. Perfect house. Perfect life." Anna shivered. Dutch scooted even closer to her.

"Sounds like you don't find her to be so perfect?" he interrupted.

"She *is* perfect. She's also a perfect brat. I'll leave it at that." Anna smiled before continuing. "Then me, the second black sheep after Bo. Finally, Mary, who is vying for Little Miss Perfect First Runner Up." Anna clicked her tongue and shook her head.

Dutch raised an eyebrow and tucked his chin.

"I just, I saw Mary becoming a little more career-oriented. Like me, maybe." Anna glanced behind them. He turned to see what she was watching.

"Closing time?" he asked, following Anna's gaze to a few bundled employees as they passed by on their way to the ski lift.

"Looks to be," she answered as her body quaked, suddenly.

Dutch pushed up from the table. "If you're half as cold as me, then let's get you back to the truck." Anna nodded and let Dutch wrap his arm around her thin frame. Despite her height, she felt tiny in his embrace. He liked it.

Once they made it to the truck, he wondered if he should suggest a little drive, to extend the night. He started to feel desperate. He wanted to spend more time with Anna.

He checked the clock on the dashboard. It was just after ten. He needed to get up early and get on the road. He definitely didn't want to show up back home just as CaitlinJo was going down for a nap. He wanted to spend the day with her.

Still, there was Anna, rubbing her hands together and tapping her legs up and down in rhythm.

Dutch couldn't help it. He began to reach his hand to her back, but instead, his hand wandered to her knee. She stopped rubbing her hands and covered his with hers before looking over to him.

He stared at her, intent.

Finally, they leaned into each other, lips parted. She moved her hand to the back of his neck, and he moved his to the side of her face, wrapping his fingers around her head.

The kiss felt like a moment or a month, Dutch couldn't tell which. The only thing that stopped them was the frigid air. He had forgotten to start the truck when he got in.

As they mutually pressed off each other, Anna uttered a "brrr," and Dutch felt his body spasm in the cold.

Wordlessly, he started the engine and took off back down the mountain toward Wood Smoke.

It was a great kiss. Another great kiss.

But, the whole ride home his attention wandered elsewhere.

***

When Dutch finally turned down the long drive of the Lodge, Anna's hand crept onto his leg, pausing at the middle of his thigh. Dutch flinched.

"Dutch?" Anna purred, breaking the miles-long silence.

"Mhmm? He murmured, slowing the truck into a parking spot and avoiding her gaze. And then she asked the question he was praying she wouldn't.

CHAPTER TWENTY-SEVEN

Anna bit her lip in anticipation. He'd given her all the right signs. His hard-headedness from that morning had long dissolved, and they shared three (THREE!) kisses together. She told him a little about her family, and she heard a little about his ambitions.

She loved that he could two-step and toss back a whiskey. She loved that he was so into his career, just like her. All of her earlier notions about quitting men flew out the truck window as they rolled up and back down Maplewood Boulevard.

It felt like magic. More magical than Danny. More magical than her wildest Vegas weekend. More magical than landing the coveted spot with FantasyCoin.

The whole ride down the mountain, she wanted him to make a move. To suggest they just keep driving. Or maybe to grab her hand. Or even just glance at her out of the corner of his eye.

He never did.

But Anna let it go.

As they coasted into the town limits, Anna pulled her phone from her sweatshirt pocket. She had two texts from Mary.

Where are you?

and

Please be safe.

Anna couldn't help but smile. Despite everything, Mary truly did just love her sister. And Anna loved her.

She texted back, *Almost home. Had an amazing night. Don't wait up, Sissy <3 ;)*

She giggled to herself. She knew Mary would be relieved at first and annoyed after that. So she re-navigated into her inbox.

Crap, she thought. She never texted Bo back. Ugh.

She glanced up to see they had just pulled up to one of the two stoplights in town. There were still about five minutes away.

She looked over at Dutch, and his hands were tightly gripping the steering wheel. His eyes ahead, mouth set in a line. He was nothing like city boys. He was manly and serious and incredibly, incredibly muscular and sexy. Anna felt her blood rush through her body, but she tried to quiet it so she could get back to Bo.

Hey, Vegas is a no-go. Something better just came up. P.S. What happened with Dannielle? You okay?

Anna fell back into the seat as Dutch accelerated.

"Sorry 'bout that," he mumbled. She smiled and stashed her phone.

"In a hurry?" She asked, coy as could be.

"Not really," he answered, letting his right hand drop onto the gear shift.

Anna inched closer, cursing the invention of center consoles.

At last, they turned onto the Wood Smoke drive and slowed to a stop.

Dutch shifted into park but paused. Anna took her opportunity.

Mirroring his earlier move, she slipped her hand onto his thigh and asked the question she knew the answer to.

"What do you say we finish this in your room?" She cocked her head and sucked her cheeks into her teeth, setting her jaw and pouting her lips.

Dutch didn't look at her right away, and he kept his hands fixed on the steering wheel. She began to tense, her mouth parting and her hand relaxing on his worn jeans, his toned thigh flexing in response.

Moments passed, and Anna grew nervous. Finally, she furrowed her brow and slipped her hand back onto her own lap. She didn't know what to say. Why wasn't he answering? Why wouldn't he even look at her? Was he unused to women propositioning him? She had a hard time believing that.

Suddenly, the day and night flashed through her mind like a movie reel. That morning was rough. Really rough. But Dutch had done a 180. He agreed to go to the bar. He drank and danced with her. He kissed her three times! They talked, but they were also quiet together. That was a good thing, Anna thought. When you can't just sit and be quiet with someone, then you know you're in trouble. But they were comfortable being quiet together. It was different. Nice. Quiet. For once in her life, she had had a quiet Saturday night.

She looked away, her eyes filling with tears that threatened to splash through her heavy mascara and down her rouged cheeks.

She refused to ask again or clarify or prompt him or whatever.

But he finally cleared his throat and relaxed his hand onto her thigh.

Anna turned to look at him, a single tear spilling over her eyelid and streaking down her face.

"Anna," he started, looking at her hard. He moved his hand from her leg to under her chin. With his thumb, he smudged the tear into her jawline.

A smile crept back into her face and he leaned into her, kissing her, chastely.

It felt a little different, but she thought that was his answer.

She leaned back, a hope filling her heart again. Just before she turned to open the door for herself, he stopped her, his hand on her arm this time.

"Anna, I don't think that's a good idea."

***

Anna nearly screamed at him. Nearly kicked and punched her way out of the truck, tearing up the front deck and fumbling with her key before falling through the front door, ignoring Dutch's pleas as they drifted through the air behind her.

She tripped her way up the stairs, tears rolling down her face and tucking themselves into the hollows of her neck and collarbones.

This had never happened to her before. Not since high school and Danny's big cop-out. Not since the scariest week of her life had she been rejected by a man. The bad feelings came pouring back in. She had put herself out there against everything she said she was going to do. Mary had warned her not to go. To stay true to her plan.

And she went. And she failed.

Anna did everything in her power to contain the sobs until she unlocked Mary's room and closed the door behind her.

It was pitch black, but she could hear her little sister snoring softly from the bed.

Her face wet, and her throat clenched, Anna peeled her jeans and sweatshirt off and felt her way to the bathroom, where she reached around the door for Mary's old, tatty robe. She pulled it on, fumbling with the tie before finally crawling into bed and burying her streaky face in the pillow. She didn't care if she stained it. She'd buy Mary a new pillowcase.

Finally, she sobbed. Hard. Not a minute into her breakdown, Mary shot up, half-asleep.

"Anna?" she loud-whispered through the dark room and above Anna's convulsing body.

Mary finally felt her way over to Anna and woke up enough to piece together that Anna was back and crying.

"What happened, Ann?" Mary huddled down near the pillow that covered Anna's head. "Anna, what happened?" She tried to pry the pillow from Anna's ice-cold clutch.

Anna just kept crying. Mary cuddled down next to her older, taller sister and wrapped her arm around her waist, repeating "Shh" and "It'll be okay," over and again until at last Anna released her grip on the pillow and slipped a hand under to rub her face. Mary took the opportunity to gently lift the pillow away from her sister's face, propping it underneath herself.

Anna couldn't make out Mary's features in the dark of the room, but she could see her silhouette looming over her, and she could feel her comfort.

"You wanna talk about it?" Mary asked as Anna let out a shaky sigh.

"Dutch… McCree… is… a..." Anna started through hiccoughing spurts, "freak-ing… jerk," she finished, sighing out the last syllable.

Anna felt Mary spring back up, the blanket bunching down below her waist.

"What did he do to you!" Mary all but shouted. Anna tugged the blanket back up and had the wherewithal to shush her sister.

"Nothing," Anna hissed. "That's what." And she started crying once again.

Mary slowly lay back down. Anna could feel Mary watching her in the dark.

"Oh," she answered, understanding exactly what had happened. "Shh, Anna, it's okay." Mary tickled Anna's hairline and patted her head in alternating attempts to calm her.

Finally, after another round, Anna pulled it together.

"I want to go home," she whispered to Mary.

Mary paused before replying. Finally, she answered, "Anna, you *are* home."

CHAPTER TWENTY-EIGHT

Dutch didn't bother to change out of his jeans or shirt. He flopped back onto the bed, feeling like the world's biggest a-hole. He knew exactly how his response would be taken. He wasn't mad at Anna. He had it coming.

But hookups weren't him. And he didn't want them to be Anna, either.

He kicked his boots off and dug his phone out of his pocket, scrolling mindlessly through photos of CaitlinJo and shots of his worksites. He wouldn't be able to sleep. Not after that catastrophe.

He wondered if he would regret it. Maybe he had a chance there. To change some things about his life.

He stopped at a photo of CaitlinJo and Megan, taken just days before the accident. They were sitting on the sofa. CaitlinJo was smiling up at her mom, and Megan was staring ahead. He didn't often take pictures, and most of the ones he did take inevitably got lost through the transition of upgrading cell phones. But this one was still in his phone memory, somehow.

Dutch could remember taking that photo. He couldn't quite remember what Megan was doing or why she wasn't looking at the camera, but he could remember how he felt when he caught the look on his daughter's face. The unconditional, uninterrupted love of a child.

He suddenly felt very homesick and terribly sad. He considered, briefly, leaving in the middle of the night. But, he thought better of it. He wasn't quite sure how much Anna would reveal to Mary and Kurt, and he wanted to end the trip on a good note. A professional one. He had to see through the morning, even if he didn't stick around for breakfast.

Though he felt bad for Anna, he was also angry with her. Why did she have to put him in such a compromising position? He thought he had made it very clear on the drive down the mountain that he had shifted gears.

Then again, those kisses. There was something in them that couldn't be denied. He knew she had to feel it. If his hardened heart could read it, then her needy one could, too. He thought of her wild red hair and piercing green eyes. Her full lips and dark lashes.

He chucked his phone onto the nightstand, forcing himself to close his eyes.

Sleep wouldn't come. He tossed and turned. He contemplated going to Mary and Anna's room. He even got out of bed and went to open his door.

But he couldn't bring himself to do it.

Instead, he opted for a shower. He stripped out of his jeans and flannel, tossing them carelessly on the floor at the foot of the bed, and dragged himself into the shower, where he stood under the hot rain.

After, he felt clearer. He put on his last pair of fresh boxers and a white tee-shirt and climbed back into bed. He had made a decision.

He would leave first thing. He didn't regret turning Anna down. He knew he had made the right decision. He had to be the grown up and play it cool in the morning, but he couldn't stick around. He couldn't risk a blow-up.

Besides, he didn't want to lose Kurt as a potential client.

And he didn't want to lose Anna as a potential... well, as a potential *something*.

***

Dutch awoke to his alarm at 6:30 the next morning. Groggy, he fumbled for his phone, muting the blaring chime.

He kicked the blankets aside and stretched his long body across the bed, yawning awake, the memory of the night before crowding into his consciousness.

He silently cursed himself. He was in a pickle. He didn't want to face Kurt or Mary. He wasn't sure if he wanted to face Anna, after all.

But he had to. He pulled on the jeans and flannel he'd worn on Friday, sniffing to confirm they still smelled of his musky cologne. After lacing his boots, he went to the bathroom, splashing cool water on his face and brushing his teeth before running a hand through his thick hair.

It was go-time.

He folded and stuffed last night's outfit into his overnight, threw it over his shoulder and left the room, practically skipping down the steps in anticipation.

A waft of bacon and coffee slammed him as he reached the foyer, dropping his bag by the front door. Awkwardly, he ambled into the kitchen, finding Mary flipping pancakes at the griddle.

"Mornin'," he muttered, scratching the back of his head as he paused in the doorway. He glanced around the great room and through to the dining room, ascertaining that they were alone.

Mary spun around, red spatula in her fist like a weapon.

"Hi Dutch," she smiled in return. As far as he could tell it was a genuine smile. Maybe Anna hadn't mentioned anything after all.

"I want to thank you for last night," she went on. Dutch cocked an eyebrow, unsure where this was going. "Here, pour yourself a cup of joe and take a seat," she gestured with a blue coffee mug toward a barstool that framed the kitchen island. He did as he was told and poured the steaming breakfast blend into the little mug, before cupping it with his hands and settling onto the stool.

He thought about answering her question with a simple "You're welcome," but she cut back in before he had time.

"Anna is stubborn as a mule, but I'm sure you figured that out. I know she had fun with you last night, but I," she paused thoughtfully. "I appreciate your decency." Mary continued flipping the pancakes and moving around plates and bowls and spoons and dishtowels, assured as could be. But, Dutch flushed a deep red.

She knew.

Dutch did not want to go down this road. He couldn't lie, but he couldn't reveal the extent of his connection with Mary's sister. It could get back to Kurt and impact Kurt's decision on purchasing a cabin.

He cleared his throat.

"Well, I enjoyed spending time with your sister. Unfortunately, I have to hit the road soon, however." He slugged down some coffee and stood up from the stool, leaning his weight into the island.

Mary twirled around, her face scrunched. "What? No! You can't go so soon!" She cried out. "Anna will want to see you, I'm sure of it."

Dutch winced a little, worried that Mary thought today would go in a direction he knew it would not.

"I'm really sorry, Mary. I've had a wonderful time here. Your Lodge is beautiful, and so is Maplewood. I am, uh, I'm going to leave my card for Kurt, though," he paused, awkwardly. "So that he can get in touch when it comes time to talk about building." Dutch reached into his back pocket, extracting his worn wallet and plucking out an eggshell-white card.

He passed it over to Mary who carefully examined it. A little smile returned to her face. "Perfect, no problem. I'll take care of everything."

Before he left, Dutch could have sworn Mary had winked at him.

CHAPTER TWENTY-NINE

A full month passed since Anna had returned to Phoenix. She spent her days at work, wading through emails, hosting conference calls, meeting investors. She spent her nights at home, which was entirely depressing. Almost as depressing as her rejection by Dutch. It was embarrassing, so she kept to herself that she thought about him almost constantly. Work barely distracted her. And she wouldn't even let her friends try to take her out to "forget about him."

Amber had called several times. Jenna and Jessica, too. She continued to blow them off until they stopped trying.

Bo had texted back indicating that she was fine and had picked up a few other gigs to pay the bills. She was seeing someone new, she said. Anna took that to mean no one would hear from her for a while.

Anna had talked to Mary three times. Once when she had gotten back to Phoenix. Mary wanted to confirm that she wasn't too upset to make it home safely. The second time on the following weekend, when she checked in on Anna's "recovery," as she called it.

The third time was two weeks later. Mary left a message saying she and Kurt just got back from church with Mom and Dad and that Anna needed to call her back.

Anna found it amusing that Kurt had gone to church, so much so that she called Mary back just to see how that went.

"It was fine. He was a little uncomfortable. I don't think he's ever really been," Mary giggled into the phone.

Anna laughed, too. She had started feeling normal again. Not normal enough to go out and party. But normal enough not to break into an emotional fit. She hadn't had a glass of wine or a beer or a shot in an entire week. She was even going to bed by ten on most nights.

"I haven't been to church in forever, either," Anna admitted.

"That's kind of why I'm calling," Mary started. Anna groaned on the other end.

"Please no guilt trips," she begged.

"No, no, no. Well, I mean, I'd love for you to go to church, Ann, but no. Mom and I decided we are reinstating the Delaney Family Easter Brunch," Mary practically sang into the phone. Anna forced herself not to roll her eyes.

Ever since she was a kid, her parents hosted an extended family reunion on Easter Sunday. Her family was closer with Margaret Delaney's side, and so it would be mostly her maternal grandparents, aunts, uncles, and cousins. Although some of the Delaney brood would show up, too.

The cramped log cabin would be packed with people and delicious food. A honey-baked ham would act as the centerpiece, and the table would overflow with fruits and breads, candies and cookies, and pitchers teaming with juice and sweet tea. The Delaney family and its extended members all fiercely followed the Lenten tradition so many of them would be eating sugar or carbs or soda again for the first time in forty days.

Anna had to admit she loved it. As a child and teenager, she always gave up cinnamon rolls, her own personal guilty pleasure. And each Easter, her mom would claim she had no time to make them. However, sure enough, each year a hot pan of made-from-scratch rolls would surface out of the oven just as brunch was served. Anna's mouth watered at the thought.

But, as is typical in even the closest families, the tradition had fallen by the wayside. Once Alan and Erica had married and moved out, it slowly began to die. As the cousins also married and moved away, it officially came to an end.

Nowadays, it was only Mary and then Robbie and his little family who would join Margaret and Richard. Sometimes Alan would too if his wife's family hosted their get-together at a different time.

In years past, Anna had often worked on Easter. When she didn't work, she would get together with her girlfriends and have friend celebrations. Often with mimosas or Bloody Marys.

Bo was even more unpredictable. Some Easters, she would show up on the deck of the log cabin. Surprise! Most years, she'd be off the grid. They had learned to leave her be.

Erica had become fully invested in her husband, Ben, and his family. She was all about her in-laws: making them the priority on holidays.

Mary's voice came back on the line as she nagged, "Come on, Ann! It'll be so awesome. Just like old times! Everyone will get to meet Kurt, and you will get another excuse to get out of Phoenix. I think Alan and maybe Bo will even come!" She cheered into the phone.

Anna thought about it for a moment. She had nothing else going on. She didn't see herself getting together with her friends. Not after ignoring them for over a month now.

"Let me check my calendar and get back to you," she started.

Mary laughed into her ear. "I know you're not working. Kurt is coming, after all. Don't be a party-pooper, come on Anna." The nagging worked.

"Okay, yeah. Yeah, sure," Anna finally answered. "When is Easter, anyway?" She silently flipped through her planner as Mary replied instantly.

"April 21. You have two weeks to find the Easter spirit, so to speak."

That time, Anna couldn't help but roll her eyes.

"Sounds good, sis. I'll talk to you later. Gotta go."

It was true. She had to go to the gym. Anna had added various yoga and pilates classes to her daily routine. She hung up the phone and went to her bathroom, where she pulled her hair back into a low ponytail. Then, she stepped out of her pajamas and reached for her yoga outfit from the back of the door, where she hung it each day. No need to wash an outfit that she really didn't sweat in, she figured.

As she snapped the spandex leggings into place, she examined herself in the mirror. She had stopped losing weight, thanks to being stuck at home every night. In fact, she seemed to have filled in somewhat. But she felt like she looked good. Yoga certainly helped to define her new, modest curves. She had a little more color in her face, thanks to walking every morning before work. Her freckles seemed to pop off her cheeks and nose a little more than usual.

She thought about what was to blame for the little changes in her life.

Scaling back on the booze had to have helped. More sleep, of course. Exercise, yes.

But that wasn't all. FantasyCoin had been huge for her. Coming into the co-president position had a real effect.

Kurt had begun his transition in earnest. Mary let him stay at Wood Smoke whenever he wanted (in the Stag room, of course). He also ended up finding an office space to rent near the fork, after all. Meaning, he officially set up camp. He was slow to transition over all of his responsibilities to Maplewood and delegate what, exactly, Anna would be responsible for. But that which she was in charge of, she took seriously.

The team loved Anna, and they didn't mind that she took on the role of boss when Kurt was or wasn't around. Things were going smoothly.

Plus, after the Superbowl, Anna had made a critical decision for the company, one that she believed saved them from a serious financial collapse. She decided to shift a significant portion of their shares from the Fantasycoin *token* to *app development on their blockchain*. Kurt had thought it risky. But the crypto market was looking a little grim, and she felt that it would be wise to bolster the amount of usable applications. Of course, they left a quarter of their shares in the token itself and were sure to continue to grow it through marketing and product development.

It had proven smart. In March, the market crashed, but they still had their apps, which provided footing for the company in a difficult time.

Kurt ended up throwing a party and even made a speech in which he attributed their success to Anna.

She was glowing.

In fact, Anna wondered if *that* was the reason she had made some intentional decisions to improve her health. Maybe it had nothing to do with feeling humiliated at the hands of the brutish Dutch McCree.

Maybe it had to do with Anna getting to make the calls.

And for once in her life, she was making the *right ones.*

CHAPTER THIRTY

March was as rough as the unrelenting stubble that peppered Dutch's jawline. He went to work each morning, a different project site each day. Two days a week, and sometimes three, he would truck CaitlinJo to school, be forced to ignore the irritating mothers, and then pick her up and do the same.

A sadness began to take hold. One that Dutch hadn't known since Megan's passing. He slowly watched CaitlinJo, her merciless joy making it worse. He felt lonely and ashamed, though of what he couldn't tell.

His parents continued nagging him to go out on dates. It seemed to really ramp up in the springtime as if they were transferring their own spring fever onto him.

Finally, it worked. He went on a date. One of the moms at CaitlinJo's preschool had a friend who was a widow herself. He didn't know the mom very well. She had worked her matchmaker magic with Debbie on a day when she picked CaitlinJo up from school.

The details were all in place. All Dutch had to do was show up.

They met for a formal dinner on a Friday night. She ordered champagne and talked about her deceased husband. She was a year older than he but acted like she was from an entirely different generation. She ordered the most expensive thing on the menu and spoke of little other than her current crochet project.

When the bill came, she batted her eyelashes and dabbed at a lone tear, admitting to Dutch that she had never gotten over her late husband.

Dutch picked up the bill and scrambled out of there without much more than a goodbye. During the date, all he could think about was CaitlinJo. And Maplewood. And Anna Delaney.

He tried to talk himself out of thinking about her. She was moody and even a bit immature. But she seemed sincere. She wore her heart on her sleeve. She had ambition. She was stunning, but that was just icing. Dutch could have kicked himself for how he had handled it.

Then it came. The call.

He was in his in-home office when the call came in. It was an unknown number. He only gave out his personal cell to friends and family. But it was also printed onto the business cards he hardly ever used.

"McCree Construction and Outfitters, this is Dutch." His voice was deep but lilting.

It was Kurt.

"Dutch! Dutch McCree, this is Kurt Cutler- from FantasyCoin?"

Dutch took a breath and counted to two before replying, but Kurt beat him to the punch.

"Maplewood? Mary and Anna- ring a bell?" he laughed.

"Of course! Hi, Mr. Cutler. Of course. How have you been?" He allowed his tone to lighten, but he was gripping the arm of his chair with all his might.

"Great, actually," Kurt started. "Things have been great. FantasyCoin is moving in the right direction, as are my plans for Maplewood and, naturally, Mary," Kurt chuckled. "In fact, that's why I'm calling. I have made the decision to build with you. Or, I suppose, to have you build *for* me." Again, Kurt chuckled.

"Terrific news, Mr. Cutler. I'm very excited to hear that. We can get rolling as soon as you'd like. Were you thinking new construction, or did you have your eye on one of the home sites that are well underway?" Dutch released his grip on the arm, disappointment filling him.

"That's where I'm a little stuck, actually. You see, I'm hoping to propose to Mary in one of the cabins. I'm planning for it to be our *home*, obviously. But, my timeline is a little crunched. I wanted to put the proposal in motion before her summer rush, to give us time to enjoy the engagement a little. That is, I mean, assuming she says yes."

Dutch smiled at Kurt's humble nature. It wasn't often such a smart and successful man was so able to come across as self-deprecating and down-to-earth.

Dutch jumped in. "I understand totally. And might I congratulate you, at least tentatively," Dutch allowed himself to chortle at his own words, and, thankfully, Kurt joined in. "So," he continued. "We could do one of two things- get you rolling *today* with a floor plan and a commitment, *or*, I can arrange to have you tour a unit that is in progress. Now, I'll warn you that it's not very likely either option will result in a finished product before, say, June. We take pride in our work and want things to be done correctly. That said, you could consider buying one of the five models. But, if I'm being honest, I wouldn't recommend it. I think you'd prefer to have your own, brand new cabin." Dutch pulled open the calendar associated with his email address to see if Jeanette was in the office that day. If not, he knew he could count on Michael to make a run up there. Michael Erinhard had all but become the project manager for Maplewood Luxury Cabins.

"Hm," Kurt paused on the other end. It sounded as if Kurt was typing on a keyboard. "Okay," he finally came back on. "I agree about the model. You know, I'm just talking with Anna via chat here and getting her to weigh in."

Dutch felt as if a knife had sliced into his heart. The air was sucked from his lungs, but he waited patiently for Kurt to continue.

"She thinks it would be just fine to go the route of a proposal inside of even just a frame with exposed drywall," Kurt laughed, and now it was Dutch's turn to join, although he wasn't as sincere.

"Well, if it's your home, then that's what counts," Dutch answered.

"Exactly. So, what is the first step in getting this worked out?" Kurt asked, turning serious.

Dutch was impressed at Kurt's assuredness. He had never felt that way before he popped the question to Megan.

"Well, I can have either Jeanette or possibly Michael Erinhard meet you at the site to hammer out the details," he offered.

"I was hoping to make this work while I'm in Phoenix. I don't want to raise Mary's suspicions, actually." Dutch was about to respond that they could handle the transaction by email and fax if need be, but Kurt jumped back in. "You know what, Dutch? Do you think you'd be able to swing by my offices in Downtown Phoenix sometime today?"

Dutch stilled. He could and should have Jody handle this for him.

This was not about finalizing details for a site build. This was a chance to see Anna.

CHAPTER THIRTY-ONE

*D*on't go with model. Mary will get the picture even if the house isn't finished, Anna typed out in the chat box before clicking back to her spreadsheets. She had taken on the job of going over their recent audit and needed to concentrate.

She had finally come to peace with Kurt and Mary's relationship. She was truly happy for them. She was. But for now, she needed to crunch numbers. The audit was routine enough, but like with any start-up, it was vital to be on top of everything. She didn't trust their new-hire financial officer enough to pass this off. And Anna was good with numbers. Very good.

She clicked away, alternating between her calculator and the spreadsheet. She already had their finance program run everything. This was just a backup report.

Anna had slowly become used to Kurt asking her for help on all things Mary. What to get her for Valentine's Day. What to send her for "Just Because." How to approach the living situation, especially with Mary's insistence that they be entirely modest and traditional.

Initially, Mary's chastity demands provoked Anna. But ever since Vegas and then Dutch, she came to see it as a smart decision, which was big of Anna. She had a hard time keeping her hands to herself in the past, but recent events refocused her. The promotion being a surprising key to that.

But even so, even with her newfound clean lifestyle, Anna felt a longing in herself that wouldn't quiet. It wasn't a primal longing, though. It felt a little different. Lately, she had noticed herself thinking a lot about what had happened her senior year. And even more than that, she was thinking a lot about Dutch. His rough hands. His boyish blonde hair set off against a sharp and pronounced jawline. He was the stuff of any Maplewood girl's dreams.

Which is exactly why he shouldn't be the stuff of Anna's. She wasn't a Maplewood girl anymore. She was the president of a cutting edge tech company in her own state's capital. She was single and free. She made great money. She had the world at her fingertips.

She shook her head, clearing thoughts of Maplewood and Dutch and opened her company email account, looking for the receipts folder to cross-reference a few expenses.

Once she did, she saw it. A calendar appointment. For Kurt. In fifteen minutes. In FantasyCoin Offices.

With Dutch McCree.

Anna's first instinct was to march over to Kurt's desk and ask what in the world was going on. Then she stilled herself. Forced herself to lean back into her chair. Breathe.

Obviously, it was regarding his purchase of the cabin. Had nothing to do with her whatsoever. She glanced up toward Kurt's desk. He was hunkered in front of his screen, a little grin dancing on his face. She didn't know if the grin was because he knew exactly what he was doing bringing Dutch there, or if he was emailing Mary. It could be either. Or both. Maybe he was emailing Mary *about* Dutch's forthcoming visit.

Anna silently panicked. She had thrown her hair up into a messy bun that morning. She was wearing a frumpy work blouse. The only frumpy work blouse she owned, because she hadn't done laundry in three weeks. She had gotten into the bad habit of swiping on one coat of mascara instead of her usual five.

She whipped out her cell phone and pulled up her messaging app. After clicking on Mary's name, she tapped out an emergency text.

911. Are you there. ANSWER NOW.

She watched the three little dots rotate through the screen as her sister wrote back.

What's wrong!? CALL ME

Anna's nostrils flared in renewed anxiety.

Can't. At work. Dutch????

Mary replied immediately. *What about him?* ☺

With that, Anna all but threw her phone at her computer. She looked again to Kurt's desk. He had his hand over his mouth, hiding a wide grin. He looked away as she caught his gaze.

"Dangit, Mary and Kurt," Anna muttered to herself. She stood and neatly smoothed her black work slacks. She felt them cling to her rear-end and was reminded of the ten pounds she had gained. She accidentally kicked and nearly tripped over her desk leg as she made her way through the office and into the outer common area restrooms.

She could feel Kurt watching her as she left, and she wanted to haul off and slap him. But, of course, she held back.

Once in the bathroom, she gave herself a once-over in the mirror. She pulled out a few face-framing tendrils and pinched the apples of her cheeks to add color. Her mother had taught the girls to do that, but Anna had never really used it. She never needed to. She was usually done up to the nines.

Anna then checked her teeth and did a slow spin in front of the mirror, assessing her body. The shirt looked less frumpy than it used to, in fact. The extra weight in her hips and chest helped give it shape. She silently thanked the extra poundage after all.

She left the restroom and bee-lined for the in-office coffee bar, where she poured herself a cup of water. She took a long pull of water then breathed out. If yoga had taught her anything, it was the magic of deep breaths.

Finally, she slowly made her way to Kurt.

"Kurt," she started, batting her eyelashes disingenuously.

He smiled at her and rose, tucking his hands into his pants pockets.

"Anna?"

"I see you added Dutch McCree to your *shared* calendar. Couldn't you have handled your personal purchase outside of work hours? As co-president, I may have to reprimand you for an ethics violation," she teased, withholding the conflict that brewed inside her.

Kurt let out a long sigh in response before chuckling.

"This is a business transaction, actually, Anna. Seeing that I'll be using the Maplewood Cabin as a home office in addition to, well, a *home*, I figured I could square things away here, in person. I didn't want to waste time and energy emailing or faxing back and forth. Dutch can answer all my questions, and he's bringing the site plans, too."

"Mmhmm," Anna replied. "In all seriousness, I don't know how much Mary told you about that weekend in Maplewood," she started.

Kurt's face darkened.

"Anna, don't worry about that. Really. I'm going over plans and numbers with him. That's it. It's not about you," he nodded, his mouth set in a line but his eyes dancing.

Anna felt a little affronted, but she didn't fully believe Kurt. And Mary's text message told her all she needed to know.

"Okay. In that case, I'll, um, I'll be at my desk," Anna finished, sheepish. Her head told her to go for a walk or duck away into the break room.

Her heart told her to stay.

She left Kurt's desk and strode back to her own, forcing her shoulders back and jutting her chin the entire way.

Just when she sat down, the office door whooshed open, and in walked Dutch McCree. All six-foot-whatever of him. Blonde hair, blue eyes, Wranglers, boots, and a flannel with the sleeves pushed up past his bulging forearms.

He looked out of place in the office, like a deer in headlights. But soon, he spotted Kurt and ambled toward him, glancing discreetly around the office.

Just as Kurt stood to greet him, Dutch locked eyes with Anna.

CHAPTER THIRTY-TWO

He spotted her. Across the open space at a little black desk of her own. She was sitting, and she was watching him like a cat.

She seemed somehow different but was too far away for Dutch to get a proper look. When he caught her gaze, his heart thumped to life. He blinked slowly at her and nodded his head. He was too nervous to smile.

Dutch forced himself to return his attention to Kurt.

"Mr. Cutler, good to see you." They shook hands and Kurt gestured to the chair in front of his desk.

Dutch wanted to ask if there was a more private spot to conduct business, but he thought better of it.

Kurt ignored the fact that Dutch was obviously distracted by Anna's proximity and instead barreled ahead with questions about square footage, split-floor plans, en-suites, dens, storage space, walk-in closets, foyers, the differences between decks and patios. He went on. Dutch had brought with him the booklet that Jody had put together on the various floor plans they were offering, including customization options.

He tried to focus on walking Kurt through each page and every number, but he felt Anna's eyes on him, piercing. He couldn't read her when he walked in. Was she still angry? Was she still interested in him?

He put it out of his mind the best he could.

Kurt seemed satisfied with one of the more traditional floor plans. It was a bigger plan, with five bedrooms and four baths. He intended to use one bedroom as a full-service office. He didn't want it to be a den or a true "office," because he liked the closet space and a door- the two qualifiers that made a room a bedroom. Kurt selected quartz countertops (trendy,

Dutch noted), stainless everything, tongue-and-groove ceilings, and pine wood floors throughout. He had good taste.

"My two biggest questions are timeline and purchase price," Kurt said after they had gone through every page of the catalog. Dutch stole a glance to his right, but Anna wasn't in her seat. His brow furrowed, he turned his attention back to Kurt.

"Important questions. Since you're going with a hybrid, er, a mix of a production unit and custom unit, I would expect no less than six months and no greater than ten. We are expecting to have a boom in contracts come June, so since you're getting in ahead of that I would think our guys could make quick work of clearing the lot and framing it out." He peeked again over to his right. Still not there. "In other words, you'll have *something* to propose in," Dutch offered Kurt a smile and Kurt grinned back.

"Excellent. And price point?"

Dutch went over price per square foot plus customizations and they settled on an acceptable figure together. Dutch liked doing business this way. It felt personal and meaningful. He made a mental note to consider providing personal transactions in the future. It seemed to work well.

As they finished up with the figures, Dutch asked Kurt if he wanted Jody to email the contract. Kurt replied that email would be perfect. He rose to pull his wallet out and fish around for a business card.

Dutch glanced again to the right, and Kurt followed his gaze. Dutch turned his head back and Kurt busied himself with pulling open the various flaps of leather.

Dutch heard the echo of high heels on tile behind him.

He whipped his head around behind him, twisting in the chair as he did.

It was Anna. She was holding a pen between her teeth and grinning with one side of her mouth. Her hair was in tangles on top of her head. She wore little makeup and he could have sworn her body had morphed into that of Jessica Rabbit. Her hips swelled out from a slight waist and her blouse hugged all the right places.

Dutch felt himself begin to break out in a sweat. He swallowed hard.

"Anna?" He anxiously stood, opening himself to her.

"How've you been, Mr. McCree?" Her voice was even, but she was biting her lip.

Dutch cleared his throat.

"Been good, been real good. How about you?" he drawled.

"Same, mostly. What brings you here?" It was obvious she was playing dumb. She was a bad liar. He liked it.

"I was settling arrangements to have Mr. Cutler here make a purchase on a home in Maplewood Luxury Cabins. But, I have to be on my way back to Scottsdale. I'm set to pick up," he paused, catching Anna's face change. "Pick up some materials for another project," he finished.

"That's too bad," Kurt jumped in, his voice earnest. "But, we understand. In that case, Anna, maybe you can walk our guest out to his car?"

Anna's eyes fluttered at Kurt.

Composing herself, she replied, "Certainly."

Dutch grinned and took the business card out of Kurt's outstretched hand.

"Mr. Cutler, thank you for inviting me here, today. It has been a true pleasure."

"Please, call me Kurt. And I do hope to see more of you, Dutch."

Dutch could have sworn he saw Anna mouth a 'thank you" just before they ducked out.

CHAPTER THIRTY-THREE

"Well, this is kind of awkward," Anna admitted as soon as they were alone in the elevator together. She hadn't looked him in the eye yet, but just the fact that she was walking out with him had to mean *something*, Dutch figured.

"Anna," he turned to face her and was tempted to grab her hand. She kept her head forward. He noticed her cheeks were fuller and freckles had suddenly splattered themselves across her nose. If it was possible, she looked even more beautiful than when they'd first met.

"Anna, listen. I'm so sorry about that night in Maplewood," he continued. He had to barrel ahead. He had to say it. He never thought he'd get another opportunity to talk to her, and although he still wasn't convinced that dating *anyone* was the right choice for him, there was something about Anna. He couldn't let their one night together just fade into oblivion.

He licked his lips, patient for a reply.

The elevator descended and quickly arrived on the ground level. The door slid open to an empty lobby. Anna stepped out, her red heels tapping away from him. The doors began to close, but Dutch jammed a hand between them and stepped out.

Anna turned around, expectant. "Well? Are you coming?" Her face was pleading. Gone were the attitude and sass he had known mere weeks ago.

He wasn't sure where she was heading, but he followed. For wearing heels, she walked surprisingly fast. Dutch's long strides finally caught up to hers, and they walked, side by side, out of the building to the edge of the parking lot.

Dutch flashed back to the ski slopes. The tone felt similar, despite Anna's shift and that of the weather.

Finally, she spoke, her hands neatly folded in front of her. Her face had softened but was devoid of any readable expression.

"It's okay. I'm sorry, too. For how I acted," she met his gaze, but it didn't feel like a challenge. On the other hand, it didn't feel like warmth, either. It felt like a business meeting, Dutch thought.

His heart wilted a little, and his mouth set in a line.

"No need. It was an emotional night. For both of us, probably," he studied her, looking for signs of life. She flinched, almost imperceptibly. It told Dutch everything he needed to know, but he still allowed her a chance to reply.

"Well then," she unfolded her arms and set them on her hips. "It was great to see you today, Dutch."

Dutch put his hand out. She took it in her own, shaking firmly. Her hands seemed stronger now. Different.

Dutch's heart started to race again. His breath became shallow.

He could see her chest rise and fall, her eyebrows lifting in question, her eyes focusing below his.

He took a step toward her, changing his grip, pulling her to him.

She raised her left hand and steadied herself on his chest and then dipped her face down, but he caught her chin and raised it back up.

And he kissed her. Softly and sweetly and as long as she would let him.

A lifetime later, they parted, smiling. Anna ran a finger over her lips, and Dutch cleared his throat.

Discreetly, he checked the time on his watch, but she caught him.

"You have to pick up," she started at the same time as he.

"Yeah, um. I have to go. I don't want to," he said, though it was a partial truth. He never dreaded picking up CaitlinJo. It was the highlight of his day. Anna looked down.

"Can I call you?" he asked, the question he'd kicked himself for not asking a month ago.

Anna's mouth turned up, but her eyes were still sad.

"Sure, do you have your phone?" She asked, glancing at his pockets.

Dutch muttered a curse. "Yes, but it's dead." He blew air through his lips in frustration. Is your contact info on FantasyCoin's website?" He knew his way around the internet. It felt like the perfect solution.

But Anna laughed, a mirthless, cold cackle.

"I'm serious, Anna. I have to go. I'll be in touch. I promise." He dipped his head to hers and kissed her once more, briefly.

He couldn't tell if she kissed him back.

CHAPTER THIRTY-FOUR

Anna knew it. She *knew* it. Why had she even bothered? Why hadn't she told Kurt to shove off; he could walk Dutch out of the building and out of their lives forever. For once and for good.

But she got sucked right back in.

Still, she carried hope in her heart. She was the new Anna. The Anna who saw in her past self exactly what Dutch was doing, and she knew where it came from.

Fear.

She just didn't know what Dutch had to fear.

She walked herself back into the building, rode the elevator up, and passed through the common area and into her own office.

Kurt was at his desk, and he shot up when she returned.

"Well?" he asked, ignoring the curious stares of the other team members.

Anna frowned at him but walked directly to the chair which Dutch had occupied only minutes earlier. She plopped down.

"So you *are* setting us up? Mary's in on it, too?"

"It was Mary's idea. He seems like a great guy. And you two had a connection," Kurt persuaded.

"Well, he had to leave. Like, all of a sudden. Didn't even have time to grab a piece of paper and jot my number down. Said he'd be in touch." Anna rolled her eyes and turned her head toward the window at the far left end of the office space.

"Here. Why don't you just take the bull by the horns? You do it all the time at work. On the weekends."

Dutch pressed a little white rectangle across the table and to her.

She picked it up. It was Dutch's business card.

Anna stared at the card, noting the company name. *McCree Construction and Outfitters*. It sounded like something out of a western movie. She liked it.

She liked Dutch, too.

But the ball was in his court.

"Thanks, but no thanks, Kurt." She handed him back the card. "I think it's best if he makes good on his promise. And if I, for once, just see what happens.

Anna left and decided to take her lunch break.

As she re-entered the elevator, she pulled her phone out and dialed Mary's number.

"Wood Smoke Lodge, this is Mary."

"Hey Mare, nice try," Anna sighed into the phone.

"Ann? What do you mean?"

"Let's just say, I'm not going to hold my breath."

The two rehashed the scene out at the parking lot, Mary analyzing every aspect, commenting on the weirdness of him kissing her out of the blue and then dipping out. Finally, Mary said what Anna needed to hear.

"Well, he's a good guy, Anna. I think he's gonna call. But you're right to try and move on for now. Set him out of your brain. See what the next week brings. Start thinking about what you're going to make for Easter Brunch."

"I have to *make* something?" Anna whined.

"Or just buy something, re-plate it, and bring it?" Mary offered, recalling Anna's aversion to cooking, baking, and any other kitchen tasks.

"Fine." Anna clicked the speaker icon so that she could do some web browsing on Easter dishes as she sat down with her salad and sparkling water in the building's cafeteria.

Mary was babbling on about Kurt and how things were generally going well, but she was a little worried that he hadn't found a place to live yet, and he needed to start being more mindful of that or else Mom and Dad would start wondering… when an email came through to Anna's work inbox.

She didn't recognize the address- *willliam@mco.com*

Anna interrupted her sister's ongoing chatter. "Mare, stop talking. I need to read this."

CHAPTER THIRTY-FIVE

"*Anna, it was great to see you today. I'd love to take you out for dinner whenever you're free. Please call me at the number below. — Dutch,*" his secretary read over the phone.

"Sounds perfect, Jody. Send it. And thanks." Dutch hit END on the call.

Once Dutch had gotten into his truck, he dug through the console and, miraculously, found an extra cell charger. He jammed it into his phone. Briefly, he considered running back into the office building and tracking Anna down for her number. But he just didn't have time. His parents were at doctors' appointments all afternoon- they were unavailable. He had to get CaitlinJo.

So, he scrambled. As he drove through the heavy midday traffic, his phone slowly picked up a little charge allowing him to call Jody and directed her through searching for FantasyCoin's website, finding Anna's email (Jody said no phone number was listed), and shooting over something before it was too late.

As he pulled onto the freeway that would connect him to Scottsdale, he breathed a sigh of relief.

Even if it went nowhere. Even if they were incompatible or if he realized he was right- and he shouldn't date anyone, Dutch felt that he had made the decision that he should be making.

By the time he made it to the preschool, dismissal was underway, so he jumped out of the truck and jogged up to the front office.

"Daddy!" CaitlinJo squealed from the little bench by the desk.

"I'm so sorry I'm late, baby girl." He picked up his daughter and snuggled her against him, kissing her head half a dozen times before waving to the secretary and dipping back outside.

It was a warm day. It felt like he was smack dab in the middle of spring. Almost swimming weather. He wondered what the weather was like in Maplewood.

After buckling CaitlinJo into her car seat, he let her ramble away about her day. As she gave him the highlights (nobody in the class had an accident at all!) and lowlights (Steven R. puked after he drank two cartons of chocolate milk during snack time), he felt a pang of guilt.

Why hadn't he just told Anna it was his own little daughter he had to pick up? What was the big deal? He had never kept CaitlinJo a secret. She was the light of his life. In fact, he was surprised that Michael hadn't made mention of her. Certainly, if he had, CaitlinJo would have come up in conversation by then.

Was Dutch ashamed of being a father? Certainly not. Not only was he proud to be a dad, but he was also proud of the little girl he was raising.

But try as he might, he simply couldn't see a future that had room for anyone other than CaitlinJo and him. Telling Anna about CaitlinJo would make his relationship with her- romantic or not- real.

As soon as they arrived home, CaitlinJo careened through the house, disappearing into her princess bedroom for nap. She slept in bed with Dutch after Megan's death and had only just recently taken it upon herself to sleep in her big-girl bed.

Dutch missed cuddling, but he was happy to have a moment alone. He had to check his phone.

He peeked his head into her pink room to see CaitlinJo tucked neatly under yellow sheets and a white afghan Meemaw had made for her.

After closing the door as softly as possible, he padded down the hallway and into his office, where he closed that door, too.

Finally, he pulled out his phone, which still had only a 15% charge. No missed calls. One unread text.

He opened his messaging app as fast as his oversized thumb would allow.

It was from an unknown number with a familiar-but-foreign area code. He clicked it open.

Hi. This is Anna. Dinner sounds great. Tonight? How's 7?

Dutch's heart raced and blood coursed up his neck and out his limbs. He felt like a child at Christmastime. He wasn't sure why she hadn't called instead of texted, but he didn't care. He could text, too.

Terrific, he typed out but paused. Seven was pretty late for dinner, especially if he'd have to pick her up and bring her back home. Even if they met somewhere, which he wouldn't hear of, he wouldn't be home until at least ten o'clock. Probably later. He hadn't asked his parents if they could watch CaitlinJo, and he wasn't sure he wanted to be out so late at night.

He rubbed at his jaw and considered his options. A. Affront Anna further by declining altogether. B. Look like an old man and ask to bump up the time (at the risk that she couldn't go earlier). C. Ask for a rain check or suggest a different night.

All of them could be a risk, especially with this mercurial woman.

Dutch sat down in his chair, laying the phone on his thigh while he laced his fingers and stretched his hands out.

He had only one choice. He had to make it work.

He returned to his drafted message.

Terrific. Where should I pick you up?

Hitting send was surprisingly easy. But a pit formed in his stomach after. He quickly clicked over to his contacts and dialed up his mom.

She answered on the third ring. "Hi, Dutch. We're just leaving Dr. Fiorillo's office. She gave us both a clean bill of health. Of course, Bill needs to start taking his blood pressure medication again, but I already *knew* that," his mother droned on as if they were in the middle of a conversation. Then he heard his dad on the other end of the line, griping at Debbie for nagging him and accusing her of not having a medical degree or a license to practice. Dutch had to laugh.

"Mom?" he tried to refocus her. "Mom? I need to ask a favor."

"Oh sure, hon. Anything. Although tomorrow I'm going to water aerobics at 6am, so if it's…"

"No, no. It's for tonight," Dutch cut her off. "I have, um. I have an appointment. At seven. Can you two watch CaitlinJo? I can bring her there or you can come here. I might be out pretty late. It's a dinner with a client, actually." There he went again, lying. Dutch almost couldn't control it. He decided to backpedal. "Actually, Mom. It's a date." He braced for impact.

"A DATE?!" Debbie McCree screeched into the phone and went on a five-minute rant that could rival any soap opera mom ever.

When she had finally calmed, he gave her few details. Seven pm, but they'd have to come earlier since it would be a bit of a drive for him. No, he didn't know where he was taking her. No, Red Lobster probably wouldn't be a good idea, but thanks. No, it was not the widow. Different.

Dutch hung up and rubbed his jaw.

Different.

CHAPTER THIRTY-SIX

Anna sped home from work and *might* have run a stop sign. Or, at least, rolled through one. As soon as she pulled up to her two-bedroom on Portland St., she dashed inside, frantic.

Shower, shave, hair, makeup, lotion, dress. In that order. Or maybe she'd dress before hair. Whatever.

She scrambled into her walk-in shower, scalding herself at first. Twenty minutes and a steam-filled bathroom later, she stepped out, blotting away the droplets from her creamy skin. She lotioned up and opted for her silk bathrobe.

Next came hair. Anna's hair was insane. Blow-drying it meant frizz. Air-drying it meant frizz. She had to do a delicate dance of a low-heat blowout with lots of product and lots of scrunching before she ended up with something that would pass.

As she flipped her reddish hair up and back and examined it in the mirror, she was surprisingly satisfied. She had achieved a bit of the Julia Roberts-in-the-early-'90s look. It worked.

Next came makeup. She wasn't sure if she should go all in-smoky eye and heavy foundation/highlighting/contouring or something more natural. She thought back to Maplewood. How had Dutch seen her then? Both ways, really. But when he kissed her, she was in full drama mode. She ended up compromising. Heavy on the eyes and with the rouge, light everywhere else. She pulled it off nicely, especially with her crystal-clear skin.

Finally, she stalked through her bedroom and into her walk-in, where she ran her hand across dozens of blouses, trousers, skirts, rompers, and dresses. It occurred to her that they hadn't settled on where they were going. She had to play it safe and dress to the nines. There was no other way.

She dug through the back of her dress rack until she found a little black number she had bought the summer before and never worn. It screamed "hot date," and she knew it'd be perfect.

Until she tried to pull it up past her hips.

Anna froze. She hadn't gained *that* much weight. What the heck? She pulled the dress down off her legs and splayed it up to let it fall over her head. As soon as the fabric slid to her shoulders, it stuck there, too.

In full panic mode, she shimmied back out and pulled the tag- size 2. What had she been thinking? Even at her slimmest, she was never a two. Ugh. She bit her lip, worrying that not only did the perfect dress not fit but would anything else? Had her body changed that dramatically?

She caught a view of herself in her full-length mirror. Yes. Her body had changed. But she was certain it was for the better. Her lankiness was long gone, and in its place defined arms, toned legs, a true waist that fell in between luscious hips and a woman's bosom. She felt hotter than she had ever felt.

She ducked back into the closet and came out with three more dresses- one blue, one red, and one a New Year's Eve silvery, glittery, number. She immediately nixed the silver. Yuck. But as she tried to squeeze into the red and blue, she failed. She could maybe get the blue to work if she didn't mind not sitting or breathing. But she did mind that. Very much.

Now on the brink of tears, she stomped out to the kitchen table, where she had left her attaché and in it, her phone. She pulled up Dutch's text thread and clicked to reply. She could call him, but she didn't want to start crying.

Getting ready. Can't wait… where are we going?

She bit down on her lip and tapped her foot, waiting for him to respond.

But he didn't, not right away. She took three deep breaths and thought about it before finally deciding that this was urgent enough that she needed to woman-up and call. Maybe he didn't notice his texts.

He answered after the first ring.

"Anna." She could hear him smile into the phone.

"Dutch." She smiled too, calm. Happy.

"I'm still getting ready. I should be out the door by," he paused and she thought she heard a woman's voice in the background. She could let it go. Should let it go. But she didn't. Before he came back on, she interjected.

"Do you have company?"

His voice was quick and a little higher. "No, I mean yes. I mean. Well, my mom is here," he finally admitted. Anna laughed, uncomfortable. She had no idea why his mom would be helping him get ready. Unless... he lived with her? Suddenly, she cared a little less about what she wore. But not enough to give up.

"Okay, well I was just calling to see where we are going. I'm not quite sure how to dress."

"Oh right, right. Sorry about that. Are you a meat-eater?" He asked.

She hesitated, unsure how to answer. She had dabbled in vegetarianism for the past year. But she hadn't clung to it like a lifestyle choice. More just a pastime. Finally, she answered, "I can be."

"That's what I like to hear," he replied. "We'll be heading to my favorite restaurant in the greater Phoenix area, then. Blackie's Beef and Beer."

Anna smiled to herself. A steakhouse. She should have guessed. But she still wasn't sure if jeans would be appropriate.

"What are you wearing?" She asked, knowing it would give her little to work with.

"My usual," he replied. "Shirt and jeans." And with that, he said he had to go. Anna clicked End Call, thinking over his response. Dutch wasn't one to put on airs, that much was clear.

Screw it, she thought and returned to her closet one final time.

***

When the doorbell rang, Anna had finally zipped up the pair of jeans she had inexplicably kept since just after college. Her mom had bought them for her, as part of a gift basket for graduating. At the time, Anna practically laughed. They were a size too big and they were *Wranglers*. She had given up ranch pants, as she called them, senior year.

But when she pulled them on tonight, she felt sexy. They hugged her body perfectly, but she could zip them with ease, much to her own peace of mind. She paired them with the boots she wore when she visited home, a set of leather lace-ups. They were worn, but they were stylish. Finally, she topped it all off with a fitted white button-down blouse, the top few buttons left undone, and a long, thin necklace.

It was the most dressed down Anna had been in years. But it was the sexiest she had felt her whole life.

She strode to the door, grabbing her little, leather clutch on her way there. She decided to leave her phone at home. All she needed was her house key, wallet, lip gloss, and a couple of stray sticks of gum. Just in case.

She checked the peephole- force of habit when you live in the big city.

There he was, dashingly handsome, holding a bouquet of long-stemmed, white roses. She stifled a gasp, her heart racing, and pulled open the door in a grand sweeping motion.

He waited until she invited him in. A cocky grin lingered on his freshly shaven face.

"Oh my," she started, holding a hand over her mouth. "These are beautiful."

"Thank you for agreeing to join me tonight," he answered, the picture of manners and respect. Before taking the flowers, Anna pressed up on her heels to give him a chaste peck on the cheek. He held her lower back and whispered into her ear. "*You are beautiful.*"

Anna flushed a deep red, wrapping her hand around the stems and taking them from him to the sink. She let her smile do the thanking as she hurried to fill a vase (thank God she had listened to her mother when she said to keep some under the sink at all times) and arrange the flowers inside.

Finally, she returned to him, and they left the building together.

As had become their custom, they kept silent on the drive, each apparently deep in thought.

But something was still bugging Anna.

CHAPTER THIRTY-SEVEN

Anna looked more stunning than ever, Dutch thought. He was very glad he went for it. And, although he didn't tell CaitlinJo that he was going on a date, she called out, "Good luck, Daddy!" as he was leaving. And he felt lucky, for sure.

On the drive to Blackie's, he began to imagine a different future for the first time in two years. It was as though Anna had breathed new life into his world. Seeing her in the office in her heels and no-nonsense business outfit furthered his passion, but the view of her framed by her doorway in a white top and jeans... that solidified it. He was officially interested. He hoped that over dinner they would move past the first kiss/second kiss stage and talk. Seriously.

But as soon as they'd arrived at the restaurant, Dutch detected what he thought was a subtle shift. Anna didn't wait for him to open the door, but she did let him hold her hand when they walked up to the host's station.

Then, as they made their way back to the table, she moved in closer to him and let him pull her chair out.

Maybe she was fine, after all. Anyway, he was dealing with a career woman, he had to remind himself. A titan of her industry. Someone who was used to calling the shots.

They made small talk over drinks and appetizers. He noticed she didn't really touch her glass of wine, which encouraged him to take it easy with his own drink.

Then, just after they ordered their main course (steak, medium rare for him, prime rib, medium well for her) it came.

"Dutch, I have to ask. And it's fine if the answer is yes. But, do you..." Anna glanced around, suspicion filling her eyes. He had no idea where this was going. Did she find out he had gone on a date with someone else? Did that bother her?

Then, just before she dropped it, he knew. It had to be CaitlinJo. Word got out.

"Do you still live at home?" She deadpanned.

Dutch couldn't help it. He started laughing. Loudly and with the full release of someone whose secret was still safely tucked inside his heart.

Anna smiled, slowly at first, her eyes widening. "I'm wrong, then?"

Dutch took a sip of his drink, keeping his eyes on it as he replaced it above his bread plate.

"Wrong, yes," he finally came up for air. "I definitely do not live with my parents."

"Oh, well there's nothing wrong with that if you do," Anna poked.

"Oh no, I don't. But," he started, meeting her gaze and allowing her to resume a leery expression. "They live down the street from me. We are very close."

Anna laughed in reply, taking a drink of her water and another bite of a fried onion ring.

His face fell, and he realized at one point he really did need to come clean about CaitlinJo, his world. His heart. His life.

But his chance had passed, and they fell into the energy that he had hoped they would. Anna came to life. She was funny and vibrant and incredibly smart. She wowed him with her knowledge of app development and digital money. Numbers and computers were her thing. He wasn't too shabby with math either, and he was enjoying the opportunity to match wits with a woman.

"So, tell me, Anna. How did it come to pass that you set Kurt up with your sister?" He shamelessly pried, interested in how that union took shape.

Anna began to brush him off, reminding him that it just happened at the FantasyCoin retreat in December. Nothing she had to do with.

But he didn't give up. He could feel the tension when he was at the Lodge.

"Really? Do you regularly play matchmaker, then?" "No, not at all. If you couldn't tell, I'm not the type who thinks romance makes the world go 'round." Her face fell a little, and she drew from her water glass again.

"Why not? Have you been burned one too many times?" Just then, the waiter arrived, placing their steaming dinners in front of them. Dutch leaned back, keeping his gaze on Anna, looking for a hint of a reaction. There was none.

Once the waiter left, she let out a disingenuous chuckle. "Hardly." She picked up her knife and fork and began to saw into her dish. "This is the first time I've had steak in months," she admitted, splashing her forkful into the cup of au jus.

"So *you* are the heartbreaker, then." Dutch joined her in eating.

"I wouldn't say that either," Anna replied still avoiding eye contact. Dutch finally let it rest, alternating between sips of water and bites of steak.

Suddenly, Anna broke the silence. "Do you want kids one day, Dutch?"

Dutch actually choked on his water and fell into a little coughing fit. He could see Anna flush out of his peripheral, but he couldn't come up for air in time to reassure her.

"I'm so sorry, not first-date level. My bad. Just wondering. Total curiosity, that's all." She looked down at her plate, her mouth set in a line.

"No, no." He finally recovered. "I don't mind at all. That's what we're here to do. Get to know each other." He did his best to offer a warm smile, and she finally looked back up, her eyebrows pinched up together.

Her question still stood. This was his chance. She was giving him an opening to break the truth. But he hesitated too long.

"I don't," she admitted, meeting his gaze with a steely stare.

CHAPTER THIRTY-EIGHT

I t wasn't true.

Not all the way, at least. But Anna had to throw it out there. She had to see how the kind-hearted, hard-working, honest, dashing Dutch McCree would respond to such an admission. Because if it was a deal breaker for him, she needed to know now. Not weeks or months into a love affair she wouldn't be able to extricate herself from.

Ever since Danny and the fated baby, Anna had allowed a metal veneer to encapsulate her, shielding her from false hopes and broken dreams.

She threw herself into school, and then into the workforce, and, along the way, into the arms of any hot guy she came across. It was how she dealt with it, and she knew that.

Then she started at FantasyCoin, and that veneer began to dissipate. Slowly at first. After a year, Anna felt fully enmeshed in her career. FantasyCoin became the family to replace the one she couldn't trust. When her parents swept her grief under the rug, she resolved to seek love elsewhere.

She finally thought she had it at FantasyCoin, between the team members who looked up to her and loved her and Kurt who looked at her and trusted her with his company.

When she saw that FantasyCoin was not going to be as important to Kurt as it had become to her, she was crushed. Things spun out of control, but her usual approach to solving her problems didn't work.

Vegas was a bust. She hated what she saw in her so-called friends. She hated what she saw in herself. A needy, shallow woman with nothing more than a job. Sure, she had her sisters, especially Mary. But Mary began to fall into the trap of a budding romance. Bo was unreliable. Anna had never been close to Erica, who was the image of a fruitful, perfect little wife and mother. The thing Anna could never be, no matter how deeply she needed it. The promotion helped. It brought it her focus and kept her busy.

And then she met Dutch, and for the first time, she could see a different future for herself. Maybe she could fall in love again. Someone who knew her worlds- both of them. He knew a small-town upbringing, and he knew a stressful, fast-paced city life.

But she didn't know him well enough. Did he see himself having the picture-perfect life that she never could?

So, she put it out there.

She looked for a reaction in those crystalline blue eyes. Surprise, relief, pure joy, even. After all, lots of men were ambivalent about kids. Many didn't want kids at all. If there was anything she'd learned during her wild years, it was that men didn't want to be ensnared in some sort of family trap. Especially a man who was already well into his thirties. Surely by now, Dutch would have already settled down if that was his goal.

But his face told an entirely different story. He hardened. He became the man she first met. Serious, erect, and unsmiling.

He quietly set his fork and knife down on the table then picked up his napkin, carefully dabbing his mouth with his oversized, rough hand.

A lump formed in Anna's throat. She wanted Dutch more than she had wanted any guy she'd ever been out with. But she had said the wrong thing. Her heart began to tear. She cursed Danny and the circumstances that rendered her half a woman. Still, she waited. Maybe she had misjudged him. Maybe he was about to say that no, no. He didn't want children. He only wanted Anna. She would be enough.

But she was very wrong.

He folded his napkin with severe precision and laid it over his half-eaten steak.

"Anna, I have a daughter."

CHAPTER THIRTY-NINE

Dutch was shocked. When Anna had asked if he wanted children, surely she was getting at the fact that *she definitely did*.

But she didn't. She said so.

She gave him no choice but to fess up about CaitlinJo, and it angered him. It angered him that he had kept his world, the love of his life, the sunshine in his day- a secret as if she was something to be ashamed of. Only to find out that Anna not only assumed he didn't have kids, but that maybe he didn't *want* kids.

When he dropped his bombshell, her face went sheet white.

He wasn't sure if there was anything to save. A woman who didn't want her own children surely wouldn't want someone else's.

He was crushed. Anna was perfect for him. For *them*. He had overcome a serious aversion to dating *just for her*. And look at what she had done! Her beautiful, wild locks turned into a lion's mane now. Her creamy skin that of a ghoul's. Her green eyes belonged to a serpent.

And yet he still wanted her.

Neither one knew what to say next. The tension was thick enough that even his steak knife couldn't tear it. He was dying to know what she had to say to his reply. But he wasn't going to beg for an answer.

When the waiter came back to clear their leftovers, Dutch finished the last of his drink and requested the bill.

Their   date   was   officially   over.

CHAPTER FORTY

A week later, Anna was still thinking about it. About the horrible mistake she'd made in the name of … what? Saving face? Saving a relationship that hadn't even started?

The next night, she was highly tempted to call up Jessica or Jenna or even Amber. She needed to blow off steam, and she knew that going out to party would make her feel better in the short term.

But she held strong and, instead, kept up with her newfound routine. She walked in the mornings, went into work, yoga after work and healthy meals and snacks throughout the day. She even pulled out the little prayers and meditations book her mother had given her when she left for college (yes, she saved it, miraculously) and read a couple pages each night.

In many ways, she felt like a new person. She was healthier than ever. She was more stable than ever. She was more productive than ever. Kurt continued to glob on praise, and FantasyCoin, in large part because of her creativity and efficiency, continued on in its unprecedented pace.

Because she wasn't going out, she saved lots of money, too. Sure, she shopped at least once a week (and mostly online), but she wasn't blowing cash at a bar anymore.

Everything was right.

But it didn't feel right. Something was still missing. Anna couldn't tell if it was Dutch or not.

When she had told Mary about the dinner date fiasco, Mary talked her down from the ledge. *He'll understand.* She persuaded. *Call him.* She urged.

Anna couldn't do that. She'd humiliated herself and ruined any chances she had ever had with Dutch. She couldn't backtrack and claim that, yes! She did want children! Her insecurities got the best of her! without explaining everything that had happened more than ten years ago.

And, anyway, even if she did want kids, did she want someone else's?

It was a no go. Non-starter.

So, Anna knew that her heart wasn't aching only for Dutch.

A week after the infamous date disaster, Anna got a phone call that would shine a light on what was bothering her so much.

"Mom? Hey," Anna started, nervous. She hadn't talked to her mother since their recent heart-to-heart. Things felt raw and unresolved, no matter how Mary tried to convince Anna otherwise.

"Hi, Anna Banana," her mom cooed into the phone as if Anna was still in high school. She couldn't tell if she loved it or loathed it.

"Everything okay?" Anna could tell something was a little off in her mother's voice.

"Well, I've been trying to get in touch with Roberta to invite her up for the Easter brunch, but I cannot get ahold of her. Is her phone turned off? Have you talked to her?"

Here we go, Anna thought. It wasn't the first time Bo had gone AWOL, and it wouldn't be the last. Despite being the other black sheep in the family, Anna could not understand why Bo was such an eternal run-away. It was draining on everyone but especially on their parents. No matter how hard Anna's feelings were toward Margaret and Richard, they didn't deserve to have to constantly worry if Bo was going to turn up dead one day.

"I talked to her a week or two ago, I think? Somewhat recently. I think she's dating someone, Mom," Anna confessed.

"Oh, I see. Is she still in Tucson?"

"As far as I know, yes. She picked up a new writing job or gig or something. I'm not sure what."

Bo was the only other Delaney child to graduate from college. Anna had no idea how she managed it. Some members of the family suspected she *didn't*. But Bo was smart. She was a voracious reader, and she was a thinker, too.

"Well, Anna, can you reach out to her for me? Invite her up for Easter. She can come early and stay as long as she'd like. Same applies to you. Your bedroom is unchanged, as you well know. I'd love to have you both home."

Anna thanked her mother for the offer. They didn't rehash their earlier conversation at all, but Anna was glad. If there was more to say, then it needed to be an in-person conversation.

After the phone call ended, Anna poured a cup of water into a little pot and set it on the stove. She'd whip up some rice and vegetables and call it a night. As she waited for the water to boil, she mindlessly scrolled through her phone. She was a casual social media user. She logged in every day, but she hadn't posted in a while. There hadn't been much to post.

As she made her way down the never-ending train of photos, one caught her eye. It was a selfie- of Erica and Bo. They looked like they were sitting in a dimly lit restaurant. Maybe a bar. A fabric booth back framed their faces. Erica was smiling from ear to ear. Bo was pouting into the camera.

What the heck? Anna thought. Bo was in Philly? Erica lived across the country in Bucks County, Pennsylvania, where her husband worked for a university. How did Bo wind up there?

She scrolled just a hair farther down to see the caption.

Tucson Time with Sis ☺ *#tonewbeginnings*

What?

Anna exited the app and opened her contacts, frantically searching for Erica's number.

Erica answered on the first ring. "Annie girl!" she squealed into the phone. "Omigosh I meant to call you but things have been so, so, SO crazy! I'm moving back to Arizona!"

A twenty-minute conversation later, Anna learned that Erica's husband had scored a coaching position with Southwestern football. It was a huge deal. Promotion. More money. More fame. Closer to family. It was *perfect*, Erica had purred. The previous weekend, she and Ben had flown in to sign his contract and mingle. She hadn't had a chance to connect with family quite yet, and she was so, so, SO sad to have to miss Easter. BUT, she'd be in Tucson before the new school year. Anna stifled a gag, but at least it explained the photo op.

Anna asked Erica what was up with Bo, to which Erica replied that she didn't look so great and was dating a real weirdo. Why weren't we taking better care of her? Anna scoffed. She didn't need Erica to convince her to call their oldest sister and try to get the scoop.

She did anyway. Bo answered, and she was her usual, elusive self. Anna asked about Easter, and Bo hemmed and hawed, before finally admitting that the recent fling had ended and she had nothing better to do. So, sure. Why not? Could Anna meet her there sooner than Easter? Maybe Thursday or Friday before? She didn't want to be alone with Mom and Dad, but it would be nice to have a place to stay for a bit.

Anna refrained from laughing. Typical Bo. She told her she'd think about it and call back.

The rest of the week went by at a snail's pace, and come weekend, Anna was lonelier than ever. No friends. No work. Even family was unavailable. Mary didn't have time to talk on the phone because she was hosting a group of late spring breakers.

So, Anna took a chance. She called Kurt.

"Hey, Anna, what's up? How's your weekend?" he answered. She could hear surprise in his voice.

"It's okay. Kurt, I'm wondering. Do you think I'm safe to take a few days off around Easter? Bo is going to be in town, and, well. I just think it'd be good to get up there. Act as a buffer." Anna didn't admit that she needed a break from work. Or at least from reporting to the office. Anna could easily manage her responsibilities from afar for a few days.

"Take it. I'm going to be hanging around Maplewood for a few days, myself. We'll bring in Dave Durbin to cover if need be. But I'm sure the team can manage. Make your arrangements, and we can hammer out the details if necessary."

She thanked him and hung up, moving the boiled rice onto a back burner. Just as she did, a text buzzed through on her phone. It was Mary.

Kurt is acting weird.

Anna rolled her eyes. She knew exactly what this was about. But she had no time for it. She had to pack.

Don't be silly. We can talk when I get to town. I'm coming home on Thursday.

CHAPTER FORTY-ONE

Dutch couldn't stop thinking about Anna. It was useless. All day and all night. It was interfering with his life. He couldn't even focus on work, it seemed. But it didn't matter. They stood no chance. Not if she really wasn't interested in kids.

He thought back to their date. It had started out so perfectly. She looked stunning. The flowers hit the right notes. They were well on their way to talking about their hopes and dreams.

And then it all came shattering down.

He started to resent the Maplewood Luxury Cabins project.

Until Kurt Cutler called him for a second time. It was on a Wednesday morning two weeks after the best and worst date of his life.

Turned out Kurt wanted to adjust his plans somewhat. He wanted two lots instead of one. Dutch told him it was an easy adjustment. They could get the paperwork drawn up and emailed.

But before Kurt had hung up, he did the unthinkable. He asked about Anna.

"By the way, I have to know. Man to man. I mean, she's my soon-to-be-fiancée's sister. What the heck happened with Anna? You two seemed to make a great couple."

Dutch stiffened on his end of the line. Kurt had caught him in the middle of a walk-through on a project out in Fountain Hills.

"I'll be right back, Jody. Can you take over?" Dutch asked his secretary before stepping away from the site to give Kurt his full attention.

"Oh, well. It just sort of fizzled. Two different worlds, I guess you could say."

"That's not what Mary said," Kurt replied, his tone gossipy. Dutch cringed. What the heck? Who was Kurt to stick his nose in his contractor's business?

But he was hooked. What *did* Mary say?

"Oh?" In that one word, Dutch gave Kurt full permission to gossip away. He never expected to see himself in this position. Getting the scoop on a beautiful tech boss babe from a local celebrity who also happened to be buying one of his cabins.

"All I know is that Anna is really into you. She, ah. I don't know how much I can say. I just know that she's into you." Kurt gave him nothing to work with.

"Kurt, do you know that I have a daughter? Her name is CaitlinJo. She's the light of my life. My priority. And, Anna admitted that she doesn't see children in her future. It can't go anywhere." There, Dutch said what he was thinking. What he was fearing. What he was praying wasn't actually true.

"Dutch, man, all I can say is that you should give her another chance. The story is a little different than you think."

Dutch scratched his jaw and thanked Kurt for the phone call. He clicked End and let out a long, sad sigh. He couldn't imagine how it could be different. Anna was crystal clear. She even started the whole conversation about having children.

He hesitated in pocketing his phone. For a split second, he considered opening up his texting app and composing something to Anna.

"Dutch McCree!"

Dutch whipped around, caught off guard by the familiar, booming voice. It was Michael Erinhard. Dutch tucked his phone into his pocket, momentarily forgetting about the text.

He had called Michael out to consult on the Fountain Hills project, so they walked it through together, Michael all business until they had finished up.

"Hey, so, have you been back up to Maplewood recently?"

Dutch was confused. Michael knew he hadn't. The project was moving along swimmingly. Their next scheduled rendezvous there wasn't until May when Phase I would be well underway.

"No?" Dutch asked more than answered. "You mean to see about Kurt Cutler's home site, or…?" Confusion filling his voice, Dutch crossed his thick arms across his chest as they loitered in the parking lot.

"That girl. Cutler's employee, you know. Ann? Annie? She was such a fox. I thought for sure you two would…"

Dutch cut him off. "It's Anna. And she's the *president*."

***

As soon as Dutch was safely inside his truck, he pulled Anna's number from his contacts and punched the Call icon.

CHAPTER FORTY-TWO

Anna lost cell service along the canyon en route to Maplewood. But by the time she rolled past the saguaro fields, past the high desert scrub, and finally into the tunnel of pine trees, her phone had died anyway.

When she was just minutes outside of town, she considered her options. She could go straight to her parents', where Bo was expected to land sometime Friday morning. Or, she could spend the night at Wood Smoke with Mary and drive back down to see Bo come morning. She knew that once Bo arrived, she'd have little time to spend with her youngest and closest sister. So, she turned left at the fork and rolled farther up the mountain toward the Lodge.

Once she got in, she immediately regretted her decision. The Lodge was packed. There was hardly a parking spot to be had. Mary wasn't joking. It was a huge group. Anna had assumed it was maybe one carload of teenagers. But no, it was five carloads of college-aged kids. How were they all going to fit in the seven guest rooms? There must be thirty of them. Or so it felt.

"No. College kids are just dumb. No offense. They are in like, five sub-cliques. There are only 14 of them. Two to a room, more or less. Highly inefficient. They're from Southwestern. They have no idea what they are doing. No offense," Mary explained as she busily prepped lunch for the rowdy bunch.

"What are they doing here? I didn't know Spring Break was so late in the semester," Anna observed.

"No, it's not Spring Break. They took a week off of classes to catch the last snow of the season. They didn't do their research though. Slopes closed last week. So now I have had to play babysitter for the past few days, basically."

Anna had rarely seen Mary flustered or overwhelmed. But she was close now. So, Anna rolled up her sleeves and got to work. Slapping together sandwiches and plating them while Mary splashed water and microwaved teabags into a pitcher, throwing ice on top, dousing the concoction with heaps of sugar.

The Lodge had never been so loud. The group was playing a board game in the great room and whooping and hollering as if it was the most fun they'd ever had. It probably was.

"Are they drunk?" Anna asked.

"I don't think so," Mary replied. "Unless they stashed stuff in their bags and are secretly sipping away. I think two more are arriving in a couple of hours. I agreed to transform their stay into a Retreat for an extra fee. So I need to throw together some activities and turn this into Camp Wood Smoke. Wanna stick around and help?"

Anna eyed her sister. "You know me better than that. There is no way I'm going to be pinned into running camp activities for trashed teenagers," she slid a few plates onto her arms, preparing to deliver them to the old farm table in the dining room.

"That's right, you *don't like kids*," Mary prodded, jokingly. Anna ignored the dig and shuffled out to drop the plates down.

She couldn't help but return Mary's jab. "So, Kurt seems a little off lately?" Anna called from the dining room.

Mary immediately poked her head around the corner of the doorframe. "What? You think so, too?" Her eyebrows pinched together in worry. Anna felt a little guilty.

"No," she sighed, accepting the glasses that Mary held out to her. "*You* said that."

Mary began to chew her lower lip, waiting for Anna to walk back to the kitchen.

"He hasn't visited in over two weeks. And he said he feels nervous about Easter. I wonder if he doesn't want to meet everyone? Too much? Too fast?"

One thing Anna had become good at over the years was keeping a secret.

She set her hand on Mary's slight shoulder. "I wouldn't worry. He seems fine to me, and I see him every day."

Mary nodded, seemingly satisfied.

Wordlessly they worked, setting the table and cleaning up after prep. When everything was ready, Mary took over in the great room, bossing the rowdy bunch this way and that and directing the flow of traffic into and around the table in the dining room and the island in the kitchen.

Anna watched her with awe. Mary was not only good at her job, but she was also good with young people. Anna realized she had no interest in being there.

Once the group had started eating, Anna pulled Mary aside. "I think I'm going to head down to Mom and Dad's now if you think you can manage here? Seems a little chaotic. I hate to leave you, but I can't deal with this."

"Oh yeah. I'll be fine. You go home. Love ya, Sis." They hugged briefly, but as Anna pulled back, a tear welled in each eye.

Mary gasped. "Anna, what's wrong, now?"

She swallowed through a hard lump in her throat. "I really screwed up with Dutch. With… everything."

CHAPTER FORTY-THREE

Dutch tossed his phone onto the passenger seat and slammed his hands on the steering wheel. No answer. Straight to voicemail. He tried four times before giving up.

He considered leaving a message but thought better of it. He couldn't stand that he'd messed up. He couldn't stand that Anna wasn't answering his calls.

Dutch pulled onto the freeway and blindly grabbed again for his phone.

Using his voice command app, he instructed his phone to dial his mom.

"Hi Dutch, how ya been doin'?" his mom answered, her voice warm butter.

"Hey, Mom. Not sure if you're busy, but is there any chance CaitlinJo can stay a little longer at your place this afternoon? I have to run an errand right now, and I might be a while."

She agreed, and Dutch threw the truck into high gear, blazing his way along the interstate and toward Downtown Phoenix.

Not thirty minutes later he was pulling into the FantasyCoin offices parking lot. He glanced around for Anna's red sports car, briefly. He didn't see it, but he barreled ahead into the building, punched the button for her floor, and rode up, throwing his shoulders back, running his hand through his hair, and popping a piece of gum into his mouth. After eons, the elevator doors whooshed open, spitting him out at his destination.

As soon as he opened the door to her building, he noticed Kurt wasn't in his desk, which faced the main door. He looked right and saw that Anna wasn't at her desk either.

"Hi, can I help you?" a bubbly voice peeped over a desk divider to his left.

He turned to see a short-haired pixie of a girl pushing oversized, black glasses back up her nose.

Dutch cleared his throat before tentatively replying. "Uhm, hi. Are either of?" He gestured toward the rest of the room, trailing off.

"Oh, Mr. Cutler is gone for the day. And Ms. Delaney is out for a few days. She's taking emails; however… and phone calls," the girlish woman responded suggestively. "I can give you her number if you don't have it?"

Dutch shook his head, thanking her and excusing himself.

Out of the office for a few days? Where had she gone? It seemed as though work was Anna's world. Was he wrong?

Briefly, he considered driving to her townhouse, but by the time he was back in his truck, it was nearly five. He couldn't miss dinner with his family. He'd have to just wait. If Anna wanted to talk to him, surely she'd call. Or text. Or email. Or something.

Once he was about halfway home, his phone vibrated in the console.

Deftly, he grabbed it up and slid the call open without reading the screen.

"McCree," he grunted into the phone.

"Hi, Mr. McCree. This is Mary Delaney, Anna's sister?"

Dutch nearly swerved off the highway. He took a moment to regain his composure, glancing into his rearview mirror to check that he hadn't caused a massive collision. He swallowed hard.

"Mary, of course. How can I help you?"

"Well, I know I'm going out on a limb here, but, well, you see," apparently flustered, she fumbled along. Dutch thought about how he wasn't able to get in touch with Anna.

"Mary, is everything okay? Is Anna okay?"

"Oh yes, she's fine!" Mary sputtered. "She's here, actually. Well, not *here*. She's home. At our folks' place in Maplewood, I mean. She's taking a few days to relax. And, anyway, it's Easter this weekend, as I'm sure you know, so she'll be here for that, and well," she started rambling again.

Dutch took his exit, calming somewhat. Maybe Mary was just calling on behalf of Kurt. Maybe he'd broken the surprise early.

"What I'm trying to say, Mr. McCree, or Dutch, is that Anna is very, very interested in you. I don't know all the details of your recent date, but she felt bad afterward, and I can tell that she misses you," Mary finally finished.

Dutch nearly had to pull over to the side of the road. His heart throbbed to life, blood pulsing throughout his body.

But she wasn't answering her phone. And she was in Maplewood.

He said as much to Mary. "She's not answering my calls, Mary. Maybe I'm getting mixed messages. But, you should know I am willing to do whatever it takes to date your sister." Whew. He'd said it. To someone other than Anna. But, he'd said it. It felt good. Like he had conquered a fear or won a race.

"Well, that's great news. Because I have an idea," Mary's voice grew grave as she launched into a plan that only a sister could hatch.

CHAPTER FORTY-FOUR

Anna pulled up to the old log cabin at the base of town and sat in her car for a bit. Maybe she should have just come up the next day when Bo would be around. She wasn't sure she really wanted to have a one-on-one with her mom or dad.

Finally, she peeled herself from the little car and popped the trunk. After pulling out three jam-packed overnight bags, she wobbled up to the front stoop, setting them down to pull open the screen and rap loudly on the door.

It swung open as grandly as a little log cabin door could, and her mom and dad were standing there behind it as if they had been waiting by the front door all day.

Her dad stepped out, giving her a bear hug and a kiss on the cheek. He grabbed her bags for her and ushered her inside. She hugged her mom and accepted a fresh glass of sweet iced tea.

Something was up.

She asked her hovering parents for time to get settled in her old bedroom, finally forcing them to back off a bit.

Once inside her old room, she pulled her assortment of garments from the bags to hang in her tiny closet. As she slid the hanging door open, a box fell down from the top shelf, fumbling into her hand, the lid safely in place.

It was the little shoebox she had kept all through her childhood until she left for college. A poor girl's hope chest.

She absently let her clothes drop from her other hand to the ground as she backed up onto her bed, lowering herself down and carefully opening the worn cardboard lid. On top was a packet of photographs. The ones she'd had developed from the five-dollar disposable camera she'd taken to graduation and the after-parties she had planned to go to. She ended up not going at all. Instead, she lay in bed taking pictures of herself posing in the dark, pictures of her moonlit bedroom, fuzzy pictures of Roberta sleeping next to her.

Anna rolled her eyes at her lame former self. At least she could go to any party she wanted to now. Then, she rolled her eyes for thinking *that*. Still lame, apparently.

She dug through the box past random bookmarks; a few photos of her with her siblings or a friend here or there; a note she had saved from Mrs. Walker, praising Anna on her good work in math class; a postcard from the family's lone road trip to San Diego.

She paused when she came to the little cross necklace her mother had given her after her hospital ordeal. She had nearly forgotten about it. Now, as she sat on her bed, lacing the dainty chain through her fingers and rubbing her thumb along the cross, she recalled how she had tucked it neatly inside the little box, for safe keeping. What she was keeping it for, she hadn't been sure.

And then she saw it. Stuck to the back of her hospital bracelet: a picture of her and Danny.

She ran her hand over it as if to see if there was any feeling left.

"We never did like him."

Anna's head shot up. It was her mom, a sad smile filling her face.

"What do you mean?" Anna asked, scooting over on the squeaky bed to allow for her mother to sit.

Margaret Delaney slowly sank down next to Anna, looking over her shoulder at the slowly aging photo of Danny with his arm around Anna, neither smiling.

"Dad, me. Bo. Mary. Even Erica. Especially your brothers, of course."

"You talked about him behind my back?" Anna's face flushed a little, embarrassed at the silliness of what she just said.

"Well, you were never home when you dated him. We had a lot of opportunity," Margaret chuckled, which caused Anna to break into a small smile before slowly chortling along. Finally, both women were laughing in deep, from-the-gut, hearty cackles. Tears streaming down their faces.

"It wasn't even that funny," Margaret recovered, wiping her wet cheeks with the back of her hand.

Anna sighed, "I know. But we needed that."

Her mom laced an arm under Anna's heavy red waves and hooked it on her far shoulder. Anna let the photo slip back into the box, and braced the whole of it- the whole of her childhood against her abdomen.

"Mom, I really didn't know that I was..." Anna trailed off, staring at the floor.

Margaret waited a long time to reply.

Finally, she laid her head on Anna's shoulder and whispered, "I know, honey." Then, lifting her head, she slid her arm back to herself and angled her body toward her daughter. "It wouldn't matter either way. We loved you then, no matter what. And we love you now, no matter what."

Anna felt herself start to tear up again. But her mom caught her chin in her hand.

"Anna, look at me. I've always been honest with my children, and I'm going to be honest with you right now."

Her sudden change in tone allowed Anna's face to dry.

"I did think you made a mistake with Danny Flanagan. But, honey, that's life. And you want to know something? You may have made a mistake, but you aren't a bad person. You have nothing to be sorry for. Everyone makes mistakes. And, so did I. I made the mistake of being hard on you, cold. When you needed me most. I have never forgiven myself for it. I have been scared to ever talk about it again. Anna, I'm sorry." And with that, Margaret wrapped Anna in a hard hug. Anna melted again, crying full, fat tears.

She hugged her mother back. "Thank you," she whispered through Margaret's graying hair. She felt her mom rock with a sob before adding, "I forgive you, Mom."

A sharp burst from the phone cut through their moment.

They pushed away from each in tandem, both smiling. Margaret leaned in again and gave Anna another, softer hug. "I love you." She kissed her daughter's forehead, and then stood and cornered the bed to grab the cordless extension from the bedside table. Anna laughed to herself. She had always wanted a phone in there when she lived at home. Now, she didn't even have a landline at her own house.

"Hello?" Her mother's voice evened out. "Oh, hi, Mary."

Anna stood with the box, about to tuck it into one of her bags, when her mother's next words brought Anna to a screeching halt.

"Who is Dutch?"

CHAPTER FORTY-FIVE

D utch didn't have to think for long about Mary's proposal. It was a no-brainer. His parents would get to enjoy a risk-free and low-key vacation (besides, they needed to get out of town for once), and CaitlinJo would get to see the mountains, breathe in the fresh air. Maybe she'd get a chance to run around in the woods, something Dutch always regretted that he didn't get to experience as a kid who grew up in the desert. Mary assured him they would dye eggs and that the Easter Bunny would hide them among the pine trees.

And, of course. Anna.

The plan formed quickly before him.

They would leave on Friday after work and stay through Easter Sunday. Yes, there was a Catholic church there, Mary assured him.

He was nervous about spending Easter with a whole family of strangers. Would he and his family be imposing on the Delaneys? Would it be awkward? Mary assured him that the brunch was always a huge, chaotic thing. No one would even notice him. Still, he wasn't totally sold.

They would stay at Wood Smoke, and Mary even offered to comp the two rooms, but he would hear nothing of it. He'd pay to book the entire Lodge if it meant he would get to see Anna again. And he could. With nine completed projects in the last nine months, Dutch was banking more money than he could track. Four projects were now currently underway, and it was about time he added a fifth.

"I'm not sure, Dutch," his dad replied to the news at dinner. "We have gotten used to having our Easter Brunch at the Country Club." The aging man scratched his head grumpily.

Dutch smiled to himself. Since when had his dad, a former miner and construction worker, preferred the luxury of a country club?

"Oh Bill, hush. I think Dutch has a great idea. We haven't really established a family tradition for Easter, anyway. Why not try something new?" She patted Dutch's hand on top of the white tablecloth.

"What's Maplewood?" CaitlinJo chimed in from her position, eye-level to her plate.

"CaitlinJo, Daddy's beautiful friend, Anna, is going to be in Maplewood," Debbie replied.

"Mom." Dutch cut her off, his tone firm. She met his gaze and glared, laughter in her eyes. He corrected her. "CaitlinJo, Meemaw is right. I have a friend who will be there. But, I also have a building project up in Maplewood. That's where I go for work every so often, remember? The mountains?"

CaitlinJo had already moved on and was talking her doll into taking a bite of her fried pork chop. Dutch breathed a sigh of relief. No matter how interested in Anna he was, he intended to play it cool with CaitlinJo.

They finished dinner, and afterward Dutch and Cait went back to their place to get ready for bed. Once his little girl had finally fallen asleep, Dutch decided to get a head start on packing.

Just as he pulled his duffle from his closet, his phone vibrated in his pocket. He pulled it out, hoping it wasn't Jody texting with an issue that could threaten to delay his plans.

Maplewood for Easter, huh?

It was Anna.

CHAPTER FORTY-SIX

Initially, when Margaret conveyed to Anna that Mary had invited Dutch and his family to their Easter Brunch, Anna wanted to wring her sister's neck.

She came to her senses, however. After all, it wasn't as if she were dating Dutch. He was just as much connected to Mary and Kurt as he was to her. No one would be weird about it. There was nothing to be weird about.

But, a part of her, deep down, hoped that she could be the one to introduce Dutch. It would be the first time she had ever introduced any man to her family. No more thinly veiled questions or comments from Aunt Vicki or Aunt Lisa or Aunt Kathy. Of course, she couldn't introduce him as her *boyfriend*. But she would have something to talk about other than work. He'd be proof of that.

She really wanted something other than work, too. And that something was Dutch McCree. Rough-handed, serious, muscular Dutch.

A shiver coursed through Anna.

She spent the rest of the day in self-improvement mode. The chat with her mother made her feel rejuvenated more than anything else in recent times, thus allowing her to throw herself into high gear.

She took a long, hot bath in the claw-foot tub, soaking until her body pruned. She scrubbed her hair and left the conditioner in. Maplewood in the spring could be exceptionally dry, and she wanted to fortify it.

She cleaned last month's pedicure from her toes and applied a homemade oatmeal mask her mother kept in the second bathroom. She found some baking soda and decided to brush her teeth with it, reading once that baking soda was a great at-home whitening solution.

Finally, come late afternoon, she felt clear-headed and clean. Cleaner than ever.

So, she went for a long, solitary walk on a nearby trail, cutting through alligator junipers and oaks, pine trees and maples. She even jogged a bit down along Hogtown Lake, a pond really, so named for an old hog farmer who lived there when Maplewood was settled.

The trail spit her back out on Maplewood Boulevard, forcing her down along the main drag back towards the farm. She passed by Darci's Café and Leslie's Bakery. She leaped across residential side roads and over soggy puddles and passed Big Ed's Market and the Sweet Creek Cabin (her favorite shopping spot in town). She was tempted to go in and grab a new blouse, but she hadn't brought her wallet.

Finally, nearly an hour after she'd set out, she turned down the lane that would take her back home.

Once there, it was getting dark. She couldn't wait any longer. She knew she wanted Dutch.

She had to text him.

Maplewood for Easter, huh?

He wrote back immediately that he was packing and couldn't wait to see her.

Her blood warmed, and she smiled down at the phone as she readied herself for bed. They texted back and forth, promising to get together once he arrived the next day.

But after she texted him goodnight, complete with a heart emoji, something nagged at her.

She definitely wanted to be with Dutch.

And she really did want kids.

But did she want someone else's kid?

***

Bo arrived early the next morning. Suspiciously so. It was not even nine o'clock when Anna and Margaret, who were clearing the breakfast table together, heard her tires crunch along the gravel drive.

Anna went to the window and watched as her brooding older sister stumbled out of the beat-up little two-door car, spraying gravel about as she muttered under her breath and dug behind the driver's seat to grab an over-sized, black tote and a paper bag.

Bo's hair looked darker than ever. Her skin as pale as Anna's. Her jeans were ripped at the top of the back of each thigh. *Dad's gonna kill her*, Anna thought as Bo tromped up the deck steps and grabbed the screen door, not noticing Anna watching from the nearby window.

"She's here," Anna stated the obvious and threw a worried glance back her mother, who wiped her hands on her apron. Margaret moved them up to brush a few wavy tendrils from her forehead before stepping up to the door just as Bo rapped her knuckles on the hard, old wood.

Margaret swung it open, leaving her arms wide to wrap Bo in a hug.

"Hi," Bo said flatly as she awkwardly moved into Margaret's waiting arms.

"Roberta Delaney, it has been too long!" Margaret practically began to cry, but Anna caught her attention and glared sternly, trying to communicate to her mother that now was not the time.

"I know, Mom. Don't need the lecture, trust me. I've been to hell and back lately," Bo's words were harsher than her tone. A warm smile even spread across her thin lips as she eyed up Anna.

"You look different," she accused. "Why?"

Anna flushed a little. "I don't have makeup on?"

Margaret shook her head, grinning at Anna. "She's in love."

"Mom!" Anna raised her voice and grabbed Bo's hand, pulling her sister back to their bedroom as if they were teenagers again.

Once they were safely inside, Bo closed the door. "Who's the guy?" She asked.

At first- tempted to play coy, Anna couldn't hide her smile. "His name's Dutch. He lives in Phoenix. He's a contractor. He's incredibly attractive." She collapsed onto the bed and held a pillow over her face, screaming into it.

Bo grabbed it off. "You hate men. What's really going on? Does he own an even more successful company than FantasyCoin? Are you looking for a career change?"

"Roberta!" Anna pushed her older, shorter sister. Bo was about Mary's height, but muscular. Naturally so. She pushed back and Anna fell back onto the bed. "No. I have no dreams of working in construction, first of all. Second of all, it's just different. Everything is different. I quit drinking. I quit partying. I'm actually exercising. And, he's cool. Stable. Like I said, extremely good-looking. Nice. Just, the complete package."

"So, what's the catch?"

Anna sat up and hugged the pillow to her chest. Her face fell.

"He has a kid."

CHAPTER FORTY-SEVEN

Friday afternoon could not have come fast enough. Dutch and Anna had spent all of Thursday texting back and forth. Or at least, he had texted her quite a bit. She seemed excited to see him. He was definitely excited to see her. But their messages were light. Neither one broached the topic of CaitlinJo.

Once he got home from work, he had argued back and forth with his parents over whether to drive separately or together. They insisted he would need his own wheels for the weekend. He told them that there would be no reason for them to be separated at any point.

It was CaitlinJo who finally settled the dispute.

"I don't want to ride in Daddy's truck. I want to ride with Meemaw so I can watch my movies."

She had a fair point. Dutch bought Debbie and Bill's SUV for the explicit purpose of them having a safe, comfortable car for both themselves and CaitlinJo. He even paid for the drop-down DVD player.

Dutch and his father locked eyes. Whenever either drove, it was a battle of willpower. Both suffered from serious carsickness. Neither was willing to deal with it.

"Caravan it is, then," Dutch gave in.

After three hours, their two-car train finally broke past the canyon and into the heavy forest. Dutch wished CaitlinJo were in his truck so he could hear her reaction to the different environment. They had gone to a nearer mountain range the year before, but he wasn't sure she had as a clear a memory of that as she would of this.

His parents must have read his mind because they pulled up in the lane next to him and rolled down the backseat window.

Dutch was careful to keep his hands steady and eyes on the road, but he was able to dart a glance over and see CaitlinJo's wide-eyed smile and enthusiastic waving. He beeped his horn three times and waved back before they slowed and resumed their position behind him.

Not forty-five minutes later, they coasted into Maplewood. It wasn't long ago that Dutch was in town, and the beauty was the same, but something felt a little different. He noted the temperature on his dashboard read 65. So, it was warmer. Some roadside flowers had begun to green. Businesses along the main drag were a little brighter. A little cleaner maybe. No more berms of snow speckled with asphalt and splashed in mud. The street seemed even familiar now. He recognized the dated video rental shop with its domed roof. And there was Jimmy Jake's Steakhouse. He thought back to when he told Anna he had gone there with Michael.

"Ew, no. You need to try Darci's. It's where the locals go for the best steak."

"Isn't Darci's a café or something? I saw a sign for it…" he had replied.

"Trust me. I grew up here."

He loved her pride for her birthplace. It made him miss Bisbee a little.

Just before they pulled up to the stoplight at the fork, Dutch rolled down his window, sticking his hand out and gesturing left toward where the Maplewood Luxury Cabins were going up. He'd take them there later in the weekend if he had a chance, but for now, he wanted to show them where it was in the context of arriving to town. They honked twice, and he saw her parents stick thumbs up out their respective windows. Dutch felt good he could make his family proud.

He focused on the drive up Maplewood Boulevard toward Wood Smoke, periodically checking the rear-view mirror to see if he could glimpse his parents' expressions as they climbed farther into the wooded town with its quaint shops and eateries and limited traffic.

Man, he loved it there.

At long last, they turned right down the lane to the Lodge, slowly crunching along the gravel, taking in the impressive, wooden building before them.

Dutch secretly wondered if Anna would be there, but he didn't see her car.

They unloaded their things and made their way in, Mary offering hugs all around and singing Dutch's praises as if she knew him well. He appreciated it.

Once they had settled in their rooms, Dutch walked CaitlinJo back downstairs to find Mary. She was jotting notes into a receipt book at the reception and gave him a knowing smile as they descended.

At once, he was both worried and hopeful that she would mention Anna.

She didn't. Not right away. Instead, she took CaitlinJo's hand and gave her a tour of the Lodge. Mary somehow made it seem as if she were sharing with the four-year-old a toy factory as she pointed out a modest basket of children's books underneath the coffee table next to a stack of board games.

In the kitchen, Mary showed the little girl where she kept the cookie-making ingredients. In the reception, she let CaitlinJo fiddle with the cash register.

As the little girl clicked on the buttons, thrilling herself with the numbers that alit, Mary stepped away and up to Dutch.

In a low voice, she said, "Anna and our other sister are going to The Last Chance Saloon tonight. Maybe you should, too?" Her eyes pricked up in the middle, surprising Dutch, who recalled that Mary wasn't a drinker and didn't want Anna to drink either.

"Oh?" he said, suspicion filling his voice.

"Anna loves to dance."

Dutch chuckled at that, but something still tugged at his heart. Anna hadn't invited him to go dancing with her and her sister.

She hadn't even texted him back when he messaged her that he had made it to the Lodge.

CHAPTER FORTY-EIGHT

Anna hadn't gone dancing since the last time she was in Maplewood. With Dutch. Now, here she was again. This time with her downer sister who didn't even like to dance. Instead, Bo was drowning whatever sorrows she had at the bar next to a decidedly decent-looking cop. Anna didn't recognize him.

She sipped at her soda and people watched, feeling a little sorry for herself. And dumb. Why hadn't she invited Dutch instead of Bo? He was the totally logical choice. He texted that was in town an hour earlier. She had still yet to respond.

She planned to. She wanted to. She just knew that their next conversation would have to do with the kids thing, and she wasn't sure what to say. How to address it.

She took another swig before sliding the glass of clinking ice away from her and hunching over the table. She just felt nervous about the whole Dutch thing. She wasn't good with kids. She had even written them off, obviously.

Anna glanced over to the bar. Bo was laughing at whatever the cop was saying. She turned her head to Anna, nodding her head as if to say, "Do your own thing, kid."

So, she did. She pulled out her phone and opened Dutch's message. She skimmed over it for the twentieth time in the last hour and finally put together a string of words and shot them off.

Hey. I'm at "our" bar. Come over?

Nervously, she fiddled with her phone, opening this app and that until an icon slid across the top alerting her to the new message. Frantically, she tapped it.

"Our" bar? Give me ten. Gotta change into my two-steppin' outfit.

Anna's heart twisted in her chest and a smile spread across her lips. She pulled out her gloss and swiped it over them, following it with one of the two pieces of gum she added to her clutch before leaving the house. She tugged at her hair nervously and slid off the chair and up to the bar.

"Bo?" Anna interrupted her sister. Bo held up a finger to the cop and twisted her body to face her younger sister.

"Hey, Ann, are you ready to go, or?" Bo peeked back over her shoulder.

"No, just wanted to let you know I invited Dutch. Hope that's cool?" Anna raised an eyebrow at the man behind Bo. In return, Bo rolled her eyes.

"Of course it's cool, and don't jump to conclusions. We're just talking. I assure you."

Anna accepted her sister's reply, knowing that Bo probably did just intend to commiserate. She was unlike Anna in that way. Or, at least, unlike the old Anna. She lingered a while longer, ordering a second diet soda and nursing it as she listened in on Bo shooting the breeze with the stranger. It was the least flirtatious conversation she had ever heard. Boring.

As Anna peeled away from the bar en route back to her table, the door opened, and the country music blasting from the speakers was momentarily muted.

There was Dutch.

In his usual getup- a flannel, Wranglers, and boots. His face was even, but in his eyes was a hint of something. Nerves? Hope? Anna couldn't tell.

She breezed by the high top table and directly up to the tall, handsome contractor. Anna didn't look to confirm, but it felt like everyone's eyes were on them as she pushed up in her own set of boots and wrapped her arms around his neck.

He slid his hands around her waist and pulled her in, their bodies pressing together.

"Hi, Cowboy," Anna smiled up. Dutch matched her grin with his own but didn't reply. Instead, he dipped his mouth down to hers, kissing her softly…slowly.

Finally, they released each other, holding eye contact.

"I'm so glad you came," she told him, her brows furrowing in seriousness.

"I'm so glad you invited me," he replied.

They began to walk to the table Anna had been sitting at, their fingers laced. Anna looked up to see Bo watching steadily as she sipped an amber liquid from a stout glass.

Anna was about to perch herself on the stool, but Dutch stopped short.

"Aren't we here to two-step?" he asked, a put-on drawl curling his words.

She had no choice but to smile and follow him through the tables to join the other couples on the dance floor, Dolly Parton and George Strait imitators among them. She took in the rhythmic bodies stomping and twirling around the floor. She felt more at home here than she did in her own townhouse, amazingly.

As soon as they hit the floor, Dutch slid one arm under hers, wrapping it around until he was cupping the far side of her back. He grabbed the other and fell immediately into the beat, two steps right, one left, spin, and back again. He guided her through moves she didn't realize he had, drawing to her attention the fact that he wasn't the same man she came here with over a month earlier.

And on they went, for hours more. Dancing and moving to hits by country music's greatest. Others periodically stopped and drank, and Anna felt their eyes on her and Dutch. They took breaks, too, to grab water. Dutch had a beer. Anna continued to abstain.

Bo had left half an hour into their interlude, but not before ensuring that Anna felt safe getting a ride from him. Anna was secretly glad that when Bo left, the guy at the bar remained. Good for her sister.

Midnight came and went, and closing time was upon them. The crowd had dwindled significantly. After a second beer and Anna's third glass of water, Dutch grabbed her hand and pulled her out to the smoking patio.

Once the cool night air hit her face, Anna felt a happiness descend upon her the likes of which she had never known. Dutch came up behind her, his big hands gripping her hips. He pressed himself into her and ducked his head down to graze her neck with his lips. She twisted in his arms, reaching her hands behind his head and pulling it down to hers, resting her forehead up against his mouth.

"Anna," he whispered.

"Dutch," she whispered back, giggling.

"I want you to know something," he started. She braced for something. "If I could, I would invite you back to my room tonight," he finished, moving his mouth back up to kiss her forehead.

She pressed off of him, gently, and looked up into his eyes.

"If you did, I wouldn't go."

They both fell into laughter, finding, for the first time, a balance.

CHAPTER FORTY-NINE

The drive to Anna's parents' house felt too quick. Still, they managed to discuss quite a lot. From Anna's enigmatic sister, Bo, to Mary and Kurt, to, finally, Anna and Dutch.

Dutch learned that Anna had some sort of significant high school relationship, but she was hesitant to go into detail at first, instead redirecting the conversation back to him and CaitlinJo.

He told her everything. From their early beginnings as a young married couple, to Megan's long-time struggle with infertility, to the blessing of CaitlinJo, and finally Megan's accident. Dutch didn't get emotional, and he figured Anna might have read something into that. She was welcome to her assumptions.

The only thing he really needed her to know was that CaitlinJo was his world, no matter what. She took it in stride, validating his struggle as a single father and complimenting his ability to prioritize in such a crazy world.

When they pulled up to the log cabin, Dutch marveled at the old structure. Anna told him it was a Maplewood original, built at the turn of the 20th century.

Dutch parked his truck and killed the ignition, so as not to wake her parents or Bo.

They sat there together, in silence, for a while. Though it was well past one in the morning, the moon shone brightly enough to illuminate the maple trees and aspens that framed the cabin. He could make out an orchard just off to the side of the property. It was a beautiful setting. What a nice place to grow up, Dutch thought. What a nice place to raise children, too.

Finally, Anna spoke up.

"Dutch, about what I said on our date that night in Phoenix," she started.

He interjected, "You don't have to explain. You couldn't have known that I had CaitlinJo. And, anyway, I can understand. Or try to." He wasn't sure where she was going to take the conversation, but the absolute last thing he wanted was for her to be untrue to herself. It was important that they laid everything on the table. He didn't want her to lie or take back what she said. "If you don't want children, you and I can still have... we can still be friends, Anna," he looked at her in the dark cab, his eyes sad but his heart full of hope. For what, he didn't know. Maybe just a miracle.

"No, Dutch. You don't understand." Anna reached across the console and tucked her hand into his on his lap. He squeezed it.

"What's not to understand?"

"Dutch, what I was referring to earlier- Danny. My high school boyfriend. Well, what happened was more serious than I let on."

Dutch listened as she related a story that answered almost all of his lingering questions. Her lack of trust. Her need for attention. Her moodiness. And, of course, the reason she said she didn't want children.

"But I do," she rounded back. "I do want children. I just, it's just that I've spent over ten years thinking that I can't have them. I've accepted that. And after the whole thing, I was very, very angry. At men. At my parents. At the world."

Dutch squeezed her hand again and shifted in his seat to look her in the eye through the dimly lit truck.

"You don't seem that angry tonight?" He offered.

"I'm working on it." She smiled at him, and he let go of her fingers and wrapped his hand behind her neck, bringing her into his face.

But, his lips only brushed against her cheek on their way to her ear, where he whispered, "You're a good person, Anna."

CHAPTER FIFTY

Dutch couldn't possibly know how much his words meant to her. She kissed him hard, feeling more tempted than ever to sneak off into the woods with him or drive off together into the sunset. Or sunrise, as the case may be. But she remained strong.

Before she finally left his truck, they solidified their plans for breakfast at Darci's. It would be a whole group of them: Bo, Mary, Kurt (who was supposed to come up on Sunday morning but changed his plans), Anna, Dutch and his mom and dad, and, of course, CaitlinJo.

Anna was nervous to meet them, especially the little girl. But Dutch told Anna that CaitlinJo knew that they were just friends. No pressure.

It helped.

She snuck into the house and crept down the hall toward her bedroom, where Bo was lying with the bedside lamp on, reading a book.

"How are you still up?" Anna whispered.

"Why are you getting back so late?" Bo replied, a little louder.

"Shh, you'll wake Mom and Dad." Anna slipped out of her jeans and top and into her nightshirt before sliding into bed next to her older sister.

"Ew, don't touch my feet with your feet." Bo hissed as she gave Anna a playful kick under the covers.

Anna pulled the little chain on the light, and Bo tossed her book to the foot of the bed. After settling for a moment, Bo finally asked, "So?"

"So what?" Anna replied, grinning in the dark.

"How was dancing with Dutch, dummy?" Bo's voice grew.

"Shh, Bo." Anna waited another beat to add. "It was amazing." She felt like they were little girls again, trading secrets and school crushes.

"So, what happens next?" Bo prodded.

"Breakfast tomorrow."

"I mean… are you like," Bo waited for Anna to fill in the blank.

"Bo, I think I'm falling in love. Is that crazy?" Anna flipped onto her side, facing her sister and trying to make out her expression in the dark.

"I think you have been crazy for ten years now. Sounds like you're finally sane."

CHAPTER FIFTY-ONE

Dutch couldn't sleep. All he could do was think about Anna. Her kiss. Her hands. Her hair. Her voice. Her story.

It killed him to know that she had given up on children because of some rotten high school kid and a heartbreaking trip to the ER.

Before finally drifting to sleep, Dutch McCree sent up a prayer. He asked for God to guide him and Anna both.

The next morning, Dutch sprang awake in his own bed in his own room. CaitlinJo had slept in the extra queen bed in his folks' room. He checked his watch, surprised to see it was already seven, and hopped out of bed, out to the hall and one door over and knocked lightly.

A moment later his mom cracked it, peeking her head out.

"Did you have fun last night?" she asked, her eyes heavy with sleep as she cracked the door farther open and snuck out, the bedroom dark behind her.

"Yes, Mom. I really did," Dutch admitted freely. "We're still on for breakfast this morning. Our whole group. We're meeting at Darci's Café at eight thirty. I'm going to jump in the shower, but I'll be over to get CaitlinJo ready as soon as I am."

She nodded her head and smiled before tucking herself back through the door.

***

An hour and a half later, they were joining the others in a back room of the homey little restaurant. It even had a fully functional fireplace roaring in the corner. Dutch was already feeling nervous, so he opted to sit away from the heat for fear of breaking out into a full-on sweat.

Mary, always a hostess, took on the job of making introductions between her family members and Dutch's, which he appreciated. Afterward, Anna stood from her seat to the left of Dutch and crept around behind his chair and up to CaitlinJo's, kneeling beside the little girl.

"Hi CaitlinJo, I'm Anna," she said, biting her lower lip as she smiled nervously up into his daughter's still-sleepy face.

Dutch scooted his chair aside and leaned back to give them space.

CaitlinJo gave Anna one look, smiled broadly, then said, "I know who you are. You're daddy's pretty friend."

Anna blushed, surprised. "And you're his beautiful daughter," she replied, before winking at CaitlinJo and standing. CaitlinJo had already gone back to coloring in her paper menu, which gave Dutch the opportunity to mouth a "thank you" to Anna before scooting his chair back in so she could squeeze into her own seat again. As she sat down, she glanced up at him, a nervous shadow crossing her face. He couldn't quite read it.

Otherwise, breakfast went well. The two groups mingled and joked, drank cup after cup of coffee and salivated over the crunchy French toast, a Darci's house special.

When the bill came, Dutch and Kurt briefly argued over who would pay. Dutch finally won out, letting Kurt cover the tip for the large party.

They all headed to the parking lot in a few different cliques. Bo had taken to chatting with Debbie and Bill, Kurt and Mary cuddled together, and Dutch carried CaitlinJo out while Anna walked next to him.

"What are you up to the rest of the day?" Dutch asked her, tickling CaitlinJo in random spurts, prompting the four-year-old to squeal and wriggle with delight.

Anna sighed deeply. "I actually have a pretty busy day. I have a couple, er, appointments I'm going to get out of the way since I'm in town. Bo wanted to catch a flick later, too."

"Appointments? What kind?" Dutch asked as they rounded the bed of his truck, joining the others in the semi-circle they formed in an empty parking spot.

Mary overheard his question and chimed in for Anna. "Despite what it seems, Anna never *really* left Maplewood. She always has business here of some kind or other."

CHAPTER FIFTY-TWO

Anna smiled at Mary's response, appreciating, for the first time, that it was sort of true. She still even had a checking account at Mountain Credit.

Tight schedule or not, she had to carve out time to spend with Dutch. And CaitlinJo, too.

She bit her lip, worry in her face. The rest of the party was slowly climbing into their own vehicles. Bo was idling in her little car, waiting for Anna. Mary and Kurt had climbed into Mary's jeep (Kurt would come back for his own car later; they took advantage of every moment together). Dutch's parents were buckling themselves into their SUV.

Bill Senior, as Kurt had taken to calling him, rolled his window down and hitched his arm on the edge of the door.

"Dutch, do you want us to take CaitlinJo so you can...?" the old man wiggled his finger toward Anna. She flushed and answered for him.

"Oh, Mr. McCree, I have to go to a few appointments today. You folks go back to the Lodge. I'm sure Mary has some activities planned for you." Bill nodded and Anna took a step toward CaitlinJo, who had become still in Dutch's arms as she combed her little fingers through her doll's silky hair. Anna put her hand on CaitlinJo's spongy knee and spoke to her directly. "CaitlinJo, have you ever collected acorns?"

The dark-haired child paused in her task and looked curiously at Anna. "What's a acorn?" She frowned.

"Well, it's only the number one way to lure squirrels, is all," Anna replied, leaning back a little, measuring the girl dramatically. "Don't tell me you don't know what a squirrel is?" She raised her eyebrows in mock disbelief.

CaitlinJo burst into giggles and squealed back, "I know what a squirrel is! I do! I know!" Dutch tickled her, which only served to double CaitlinJo's joyous shrieks.

Anna smiled at the two, a pang coursing through her body. "Dutch," she interrupted her face turning serious. He held a hand up to thwart CaitlinJo's half-hearted bats at his head. "Maybe I can come up to the Lodge for dinner? I heard Mary was making one of her famous roasts." She offered him a mischievous smile, and his lip curled up on one side in response.

"We'll see you for supper then," he answered. She could tell he wanted to move in for a kiss but instead forced himself to hold back. She did the same.

"CaitlinJo, your job is to collect as many acorns as you can by the time I see you tonight at the Lodge, okay? Oh, and in case Mary forgets, make sure you bug her to boil the eggs and get the dye ready for the Easter Bunny."

CaitlinJo nodded deeply in reply and Dutch smiled appreciatively at Anna before then transporting the little girl to his waiting truck as Anna slid into Bo's little passenger seat.

To the title company, Anna directed.

Kurt had entrusted her with the job of closing on the house he'd bought in the Cabins. She was tempted to involve Dutch in the process, but Kurt had told her there were just a few papers to sign. Jeanette had already set it all up for them. Kurt was going to meet Anna at the agency, so that Anna could get the keys and grab the paperwork, keeping Kurt in the clear. He was desperate that Mary didn't find out until Sunday when they went over for the big reveal.

Anna knew the appointment wouldn't take too long, but before she ever knew Dutch was coming to town, she had booked a spa day at Mountain Escapes with Bo. Mary had decided to skip in favor of spending time with Kurt. They could not get enough of each other.

***

Bo and Anna had gotten their massages in the couples room, which allowed them to gossip and chat the whole hour. Anna hadn't heard much about Bo, so she picked away at her older sister's life. Where had she been? What was she doing for work? Who was the mystery man who dumped her? Surprisingly, Bo spilled much of it even in the presence of the two masseurs.

But once Anna was alone with her thoughts during her facial, everything that had happened in the last four months came barreling at her like a heard of buffalo.

After their facials, as Bo drove them back up the mountain toward the Lodge, Anna had little to say.

"Everything okay?" Bo asked as she put her foot on the accelerator, propelling them up a gradual climb.

Anna glanced up, biting at her fingernail. "Yeah, yeah."

"Anna Delaney, you're a bad liar. Are you thinking of ending it with him?" Bo's forehead wrinkled in bewilderment.

Anna shot a look at her sister.

"Bo, there's nothing to end. We didn't start anything. And besides, they are so happy together. I can't imagine it would work out. The kid. The parents. The whole thing. I just…" she trailed off, looking out the window as the evergreens sailed past them in a blur.

Suddenly, Bo twisted the wheel into a dirt lot that sat just after Big Ed's Market.

"Dude, Anna. You're being ridiculous. You said last night that you're falling in love with him. So either you have no idea how you feel OR you know exactly how you feel and you're afraid of it. I know the answer. Take it from someone who's a true commitmentphobe."

Anna returned her gaze to the road ahead of her.

"I told him I didn't want kids, and he, like, doesn't even care. And he *has* a kid, Bo. Isn't that a red flag?"

"Didn't you tell him what happened to you, Anna?"

"Yeah, but."

"Anna, shut up. You're overanalyzing. He hasn't asked you to marry him. Why can't you just take a leap of faith and see where this path takes you? You know. Robert Frost and all that?"

"He's so great with CaitlinJo. I'd be an outsider. An interloper."

Out of the blue, Anna's cell phone chimed.

"It's Kurt," she said to Bo as she swiped open the text.

Her eyes flashed over of the words like lightning.

"Bo, flip around and head to the fork. There has been a change of plans."

CHAPTER FIFTY-THREE

Disappointed, Dutch returned to the Lodge. But, as soon as Mary pulled out a fancy egg dyeing kit, his attitude changed. CaitlinJo delighted over Mary's skillful approach to Easter preparations, forgetting to collect acorns for the squirrels. Dutch couldn't help but wonder if Anna would be like her sister when it came to children.

However, the entire time they were outside, dying eggs and enjoying the beautiful April weather, Kurt was inside, strangely pacing. Mary tried to ignore it, but Dutch saw that she was bothered.

After Mary's second attempt at checking on him, Debbie finally volunteered to see if he wasn't feeling well or what. A grandmother's touch, she called it.

After they sat on the sofa for fifteen minutes talking (and after fifteen minutes of Mary growing more and more concerned- almost to the brink of tears), Kurt finally emerged on the back deck.

"Mary, we have to go somewhere," he commanded, his voice militant and strained.

Mary looked around her, confused. "What's wrong?"

"I just. I need to talk to you for a bit. Can I steal her?" Kurt asked the small group of worried faces. Dutch and Bill nodded. Debbie murmured an mhmm.

Mary stepped in through the door Kurt was holding open. She was white as a sheet.

Dutch threw a look to his mother, who had stepped out onto the deck just before Mary went in. He could have sworn he saw the hint of a smile on her face. But it was gone in a flash.

Kurt hesitated before closing the door after them, leaving Mary to all but tremble.

He cleared his throat. "Uhm, do you mind if I steal Dutch, too?"

***

At first, Dutch assumed he was in for the most awkward car ride of his life. Had Kurt brought him along on a break-up mission? Had nerves got the best of the confident Kurt Cutler?

But once they were in Kurt's car and cruising down Maplewood Boulevard heading straight for the fork, Dutch realized what was happening.

Kurt *had* changed his mind. But just a little bit.

Not twenty minutes later, they had pulled up to Dutch's project. Mary was as confused as ever, but Dutch could tell she had calmed down enough to avoid tears. She asked Kurt why he brought Dutch along, to which Kurt just replied it was a business situation. Dutch had to stifle a chuckle.

Once they reached the gate, he saw Bo's little beater, parked to the side, and the dark-headed sister and redhead sitting in the front seat, craning their necks to catch a glimpse of the increasingly suspicious Mary.

In Bo's back seat were two other figures, an older couple. Dutch couldn't be certain, but he figured they must be the Delaneys. Interesting. Kurt was certainly playing this smart.

Dutch realized why he was enlisted. Unfortunately, it had nothing to do with Anna.

"Why is my family here?" Mary looked quizzically from Bo's car to Kurt, who simply ignored her.

"Dutch?" Kurt rolled up to the gate key entry post so that Dutch, in the seat behind him, could punch in the code. He would have been happy to simply share it with Kurt, but he was even happier to get another chance to see Anna, of course.

He did, and the gate slowly swung open, allowing them entry. Dutch watched as Bo started her car and pulled in behind them.

Already nauseated from the car ride, he turned to keep his eyes focused on the road as Kurt wound through the paved streets and finally to the back lane where his home site had already begun.

Dutch was happy to see the progress. He'd have to bring his parents down before they left town, he thought to himself.

The slab was down, and the house was already framed. Five-gallon buckets, extra lumber, and a few ladders were tucked under a tarp inside what would become the front bedroom.

Kurt parked the car, and the three of them exited, stretching before the skeleton of a house as Bo, Anna, and the Delaneys joined them.

Mary looked around, nervous.

Kurt took her hand and walked her up to the naked wood beams. She glanced behind at her sisters, who were thrusting thumbs up at her as they watched.

Anna sidled up next to Dutch, brushing his arm with hers. Her graze felt electric, but he didn't dare look at her. Instead, he kept his focus on Kurt and Mary, who were now facing each other under the bare awning.

Kurt spoke just loudly enough that they could overhear from their distance on the would-be driveway.

"Mary, I have been keeping a secret from you," he started. Mary smiled nervously and glanced over at the others before letting Kurt continue. "I found a place to buy a few weeks back. Right here in Maplewood. Where I can stay when I visit you, where I can work, and where, one day, we can raise our family."

Anna let out a gasp as Kurt dropped to his knee. Mary covered her mouth in her hands.

"Mary Delaney, I bought this house for us. Will you make it a home with me by agreeing to be my wife?"

Anna, Bo, and their mother burst out in cheers. Mary began to weep, nodding and holding her finger out to a broadly smiling Kurt. The group converged on the newly engaged couple. The girls' father heartily shaking Kurt's hand. The sisters forming a group hug and huddling over Mary's tiny hand. Finally, the family let Kurt and Mary embrace. They kissed chastely, and Kurt took Mary on a tour of their new "home."

Bo stepped back first and rejoined Dutch on the driveway.

"I did not see that coming," she admitted in a throaty voice. Dutch chuckled.

"I hate to tell you, but I've known about it for some time."

"Figures," she replied, her eyes on Anna and her parents. "I'm the last to know most things in the family." She laughed, too. But it was a little brittle. "Well, except for one thing, I think," she continued.

Dutch tore his eyes away from Anna, who was now watching him from inside the foyer. He looked down at Bo who pointed a finger toward her taller sister.

"She's in love with you."

CHAPTER FIFTY-FOUR

Anna wasn't surprised, of course. She could feel Kurt was getting restless about the proposal. And she felt it was probably more appropriate to do outside of the Easter Brunch, where there would be less pressure. The focus could be the proposal. Easter Sunday was sure to be busy, anyway.

Her parents were over the moon. Apparently, Kurt had asked him for Mary's hand a few weeks back, the last time he had visited Maplewood. So, they weren't surprised either.

In fact, Margaret immediately launched into wedding planning mode. She hadn't been as involved as she would have liked in Erica's wedding, so she saw this as a chance to live vicariously, no doubt. Anna was a little less interested. She looked over to Dutch, who was standing with Bo now.

She smiled, barely. And then Bo pointed to her. Anna cocked her head, her smiling flagging, as she walked over to them.

She had thought about what Bo had said. What *she herself* had said.

Anna thought about how she felt seeing Kurt propose to Mary. She felt like she wanted to be Mary and she wanted Dutch to be Kurt. That had to account for something.

As she got closer, Bo magically disappeared, leaving Dutch there, his hands in his pockets, one boot kicking at the dirt drive as if he was a little boy.

Anna stopped in front of him, shoving her own hands into her jeans pockets.

"Did you get to meet my folks?" she asked.

"Naw," he replied, tilting his head to watch them as they discreetly walked themselves through the framed house. He shifted his weight.

"I'll have to introduce you."

"I'd like that." He waited a beat, letting Anna fidget a little longer. Finally, he lowered his voice, playfully. "Bo told me something interesting."

She gave him a beat before stitching her eyebrows together and moving in to jab him with her elbow. "Well?"

"I can't tell you," he answered. "I think it might be a secret." He winked at her and Anna felt like she was going to melt into the dirt driveway. What had Bo said? She hoped she played it at least a little cool on Anna's behalf.

"Sisters don't tell other people their secrets," she shot back, crossing her arms over her chest and eyeing him.

"Maybe it's not a secret, then?" He asked, curling his lips up.

A voice came up behind Anna, startling her. "This must be Dutch?"

She twisted in the dirt, facing her mom, blood rushing up to her cheeks. "Mom," she whined, allowing for a moment the teenager inside her to come out. Anna opened so that she was framing her parents and Dutch.

She saw his smile fall off his face, a serious but open expression taking its place.

"You must be Mr. and Mrs. Delaney. Dutch McCree," he gestured to himself. "It's a pleasure to meet you." Dutch put his hand out first to Margaret, softly gripping it, then to Richard, more firmly. Anna took note and felt immediately like she was in high school again. It gave her a small thrill.

"You are the contractor on this project, is that right, Dutch?" Richard passed a hand out beside him, gesturing to the expanse of pine trees dotted by incomplete homes. Dutch nodded in return.

"I'm one of many who have brought it to life. Or, at least, started on the mission. We hope to see it come to fruition within a year or two." Anna could see Dutch was proud of the project, but he struggled to make eye contact with her dad. It was cute.

"And you're coming to Easter tomorrow, Dutch. Is that right?" Margaret cut in, her eyes bright with hope. Anna cringed a little.

Dutch glanced at Anna. She felt him measuring her, as though he hadn't made up his mind about Easter OR her. He began to answer, a drawn-out "Well…"

She had to jump in. "Yes, Mom." She looked up at him, setting her hand on his arm. She pinned him with a pretty glare.

CHAPTER FIFTY-FIVE

The truth was Dutch didn't want to go to the brunch. It felt awkward. He hardly knew anyone, even Kurt or Mary. Plus, he had his whole family with him, parents and all.

Of course, none of that would matter if, at least, he and Anna were officially dating. It was too soon. He knew that. He'd humiliate himself if he asked her to be his girlfriend or to go steady or any other number of approaches to sealing the deal. Besides, in your thirties, did you even ask to make it official? Or was it just de facto-official after long enough? When *was* "long enough?"

"Oh good!" Margaret Delaney jumped in. "I'm so glad to hear that. Now tell me, Dutch," she moved up to him and placed her hand on his other arm. "What again are your parents' names?

He was stuck. Classic mom move. Margaret made his decision for him.

Anna clapped lightly, which seemed out of character but bolstered his confidence.

"Debbie and Bill," he answered.

"And they're from Bisbee, I hear? You are, too? What did your family do in Bisbee?"

"My dad was a miner until the '80s when he switched to construction. My mom, well, she tended bar." He felt a little ashamed, especially of his mother's occupation. Anna's parents' seemed somewhat... conservative.

But Margaret smiled warmly and answered, "They sound like our kind of people."

***

The rest of the evening was surprisingly relaxing. Having no other guests booked, Mary hosted a big family meal. Anna was right. Her pot roast was divine. Dutch laughed when Margaret, Bo, and Anna hovered over Mary as she put the finishing touches on the main course. Debbie offered to pitch in on the side dishes, and even CaitlinJo wanted to help.

A small sadness overtook Dutch as he realized that *this* felt like home, maybe not in place, but in atmosphere. Everyone helping out with dinner, the menfolk kicking back on the deck together, regaling each other over stories of how they had each proposed to their wives, Dutch excluded. He could have joined in, but today was about the future for him, not the past.

After supper was finished, everyone slowly began to trickle away. Kurt and Mary tucked themselves up on the love seat, playing Uno together. Margaret and Richard left to get ready for the morning. CaitlinJo was fast asleep in Dutch's room upstairs. Debbie and Bill called it a night, too.

Dutch, Anna, and Bo were the only ones left at the expansive farmhouse table.

Bo tapped out a little drum roll on the table before pressing up and breaking the silence. "Well, I am wiped out. I haven't had this much meaningful social interaction in ages," she joked. They laughed. "Anna, are you coming home with me, or...?" Bo lifted an eyebrow at her sister.

CHAPTER FIFTY-SIX

Anna felt herself grow warm. It didn't matter that she could easily stay at the Lodge and sleep with Mary as she usually did. Bo's suggestion was obvious, and it put her and Dutch both in an awkward position. If Bo returned home without Anna, then their parents would jump to logical conclusions. Anna's newfound virtues would seemingly fly out the window.

Dutch squeezed Anna's hand beneath the table and replied for her. "Anna, you should go home. I'll see you tomorrow."

Anna twisted her head toward him.

"Really?" She breathed two sighs of relief- one for his taking her off the hook, and two that he was going to come to Easter.

"I'll be in the car waiting, Ann," Bo offered a quick smile and headed out into the moonlit night.

Anna glanced around the three-way fireplace to Mary and Kurt on the love seat. They were fully consumed in their game, thankfully. Anna had a moment of at least semi-privacy with Dutch.

"Dutch, thanks for that," she said as she looked up into his eyes. "You're thoughtful." For some reason, she felt awkward complimenting him. But he didn't notice and wrapped his arm around her shoulder, pulling her into him.

"It's easy to be thoughtful about you, Anna. I have been thinking about you nonstop. Ever since I met you in the office at the Cabins." He wasn't smiling now. He was studying her, searching. For an answer? For confirmation?

Anna knew this was her chance.

"Me too," was as much as she could offer before she grabbed the back of his head and pulled him into her mouth, ignoring her sister and Kurt on the sofa. Ignoring everything.

She focused on Dutch. The heady smell of his aftershave. The feel of his lips against hers and his strong jaw beneath her own slender fingers.

He ran his thumb along the side of her face, gently pulling away.

"I need more than this, Anna." His face was stoic now. Somber even.

She scrunched her face, uncertain what he meant. "Dutch, I know I gave you a different impression back in March, but I'm trying to…" she trailed off in time for him to explain himself.

"No, no. That's not what I mean. At all. I respect you, and I want… I want whatever this," he gestured between them, "whatever this is to move at a comfortable pace for both of us."

She was confused. "Then what *do* you mean?"

"I mean I have a daughter. Stability is crucial for us. And, I'm not the sort to be looking for some sort of replacement mom for her," he locked eyes with her, catching Anna's face fall. "Which is part of the reason I'm falling for you, too Anna."

She swallowed hard, her pulse quickened. Bo *had* told him.

But it made no sense. "What do you mean that's part of the reason you're falling for me?"

He grabbed her hands and rubbed his thumbs over the backs of them.

"You don't need me. You don't need anyone. You have your act together. That's what I mean. I love that about you. You know who you are and you *see* yourself. Better than anyone I know, maybe."

Anna's face softened. She could cry. But he moved a hand to her chin, tilting it up toward him once again.

This time, they barely brushed lips. Anna's body was buzzing. She could feel that Dutch's was, too. While their faces were still enmeshed, Anna murmured to him, "I'm falling for you, too, Dutch McCree." He kissed her cheek in reply and ran a finger along her lips, his face glowing.

They parted, and Anna looked again to the sofa. Kurt and Mary weren't there anymore.

"I have to go, Dutch," she started. "But, I'll see you tomorrow?"

"I think so," he replied and stood from the table, pulling her up with him. She took it as a yes and forced herself to smile. He was daring her to trust him.

Dutch slowly walked her through the Lodge and out to the front deck, where they paused, taking in the aromatic pine woods around them.

Anna could make out Bo, sitting her dark car, the glow of her phone on her face.

She turned to Dutch, wrapping her long arms up around his neck. He wrapped her waist and spun in her in a circle before kissing her lightly on the cheek and setting her back down on the wooden deck.

"Are you going to tell CaitlinJo?" It fell out of her mouth. She couldn't help it. She had never felt this way about a man. Anna saw a future for them, unfolding before her. A sense of panic shot through her, threatening to burst her fragile, creamy skin. She needed something firmer from him. CaitlinJo was clearly crucial, and Anna had to suggest that CaitlinJo was important to *her*, too.

"Is there something she needs to know?" he deadpanned, a teasing smirk lighting his face.

Something deep within Anna burned. She didn't know if it was a reaction to his cocksure attitude or the withholding of his commitment or her own need for control. She knew what he was asking, but the sovereign woman inside her screamed out, leaving Anna to respond in her own elusive way. She couldn't be the one to show her hand.

"I guess time will tell."

And with that, she pranced off the deck and into Bo's rusty little   two-seater.

CHAPTER FIFTY-SEVEN

Again, Dutch hadn't slept well at Wood Smoke Lodge. Of course, it had nothing to do with the accommodations. A peacefully sleeping CaitlinJo was proof of that.

He had no idea what Anna meant the night before. Did she *want* him to wait to tell CaitlinJo? Did she expect him to tell CaitlinJo? And what was it that he was supposed to tell CaitlinJo, anyway?

Dutch was confused. And he still wasn't certain about whether to go to the brunch. Not after Anna's ambiguity.

He got ready for the day as if it were any other Easter Sunday- a crisp blue Oxford button-down and khakis. He then gently woke his sleeping princess.

"Caitie, wake up, baby," he whispered through her dark tendrils.

CaitlinJo hated being woken early. She preferred to get up of her own volition. She had even told Dutch that whenever he had to wake her up, he could only do it if he whispered.

She yawned and rubbed her eyes with her little fists, stretching her body slowly.

"Daddy? Did the Easter Bunny come?"

Dutch grinned. He was thankful to have his mother help with that. The basket was filled beautifully and arranged carefully atop the chunky oak dresser. "Yes, sweetheart. Let's see what he got you!"

"But Daddy, what about eggs? Did he hide them?"

Mary had handled that. She told him she was happy to set up a private egg hunt for CaitlinJo.

"I don't know," he fibbed to his young daughter. "I guess we'll just have to get dressed and go look outside."

CaitlinJo delicately unpacked her white little basket, admiring the crayons and paints, the costume jewelry and the springtime nightgown rolled up inside. A special edition Easter Barbie peeked out from the back of the basket, which CaitlinJo brightly oohed and ahhed over. Dutch had another big surprise for her at home: a handcrafted, wooden dollhouse that would fit nearly her entire, extensive Barbie collection.

Finally finished, Dutch helped his daughter into her white lace Easter dress. No matter if they were going to the Delaney family brunch or not, they were sure as heck attending the local Easter Service.

Mary had already given them directions to the nearest Catholic Church, and Debbie and Bill were to meet him in the foyer by 8:30 sharp in order to head over.

Their plans for after the service, however, were still unclear. His parents and CaitlinJo were excited to join the big Delaney family. Yet, Dutch was nervous as could be. It felt like a serious commitment.

***

Once Dutch and CaitlinJo headed downstairs, it was eight sharp. Mary peeked her head out from the kitchen. She was sipping coffee and dressed in a simple, pale yellow dress. She offered a quick breakfast of oatmeal or eggs, but Dutch shook his head. They would wait until after Communion.

"CaitlinJo, I'm pretty sure I noticed something popping out beneath the pine needles this morning. Why don't you go check for me, okay?"

The little girl grabbed her father's hand and yanked him to the back deck, where he opened the door and joined her in exploring the immediate area for a dozen colorful eggs.

After they wrapped up their search, CaitlinJo set about recounting her collection with her grandparents at the dining room table.

"No breakfast… I take it you're going to the brunch?" Mary asked, rinsing her mug and setting it in the sink alongside Dutch's.

"Not quite sure, Mary," he admitted. "I can't read your sister as well as I thought."

Mary chuckled. "No one can," she said. "But, Dutch. You must know how much she is interested in you. You should go. Besides, it's Easter. What else are you all going to do? No restaurant will be open today. You have to eat," she prodded.

"Well, we are going to Mass first. I think we have time to figure it out."

CHAPTER FIFTY-EIGHT

After a church service Bo insisted was ten minutes too long, the three Delaney women busily prepared the ham and sides, brewed the sweet tea and set the table. Margaret insisted on fresh flowers from her garden, sending Anna out to cut them.

Guests had already started arriving. Robbie and his family, Alan and his. Margaret's sister, Irma and her husband and children. Margaret's elderly mother and father arrived too.

Anna took her time in the garden, breathing in the sweet aromas that had begun to fill the air. She loved it when Easter came later in the season. It really felt like Easter to her, especially here, in Maplewood, where it wasn't too warm or too cold. Just right.

As she poked around the different plants, she thought back to the night before.

Had she been too brash? Too vague or mysterious? She didn't mean to be. She craned her neck to watch as another car pulled into the drive.

Mary and Kurt. They'd gone back up to the Lodge after church.

She sighed.

Was he even coming?

Anna secretly watched Kurt grab a bouquet of flowers from the backseat and balance it on a dish Mary had brought before opening her door and holding her hand all the way up to the front porch.

She expected Dutch's truck and his parents' SUV to pull up right after. Especially since Mary told her they had only booked through Sunday.

Anna snapped the last stem of a purple tulip, stood, wiped the woodchips from her knees and followed Mary and Kurt inside to the now-noisy cabin.

Laughter and joy filled the air, and despite the cramped quarters, it felt comfortable and perfect.

On her way to ask Mary her burning question, she was stopped by relative after relative. Hugs and kisses, questions and compliments.

Finally, after peeling herself away from Aunt Irma, she popped through to the far end of the small living room, where Mary was showing her ring off to Robbie's and Alan's daughters.

"Mary," Anna interrupted, her voice low. "Are they coming?"

Mary looked at her older sister through pleading eyes. She shook her head and lifted her shoulders.

She didn't know.

She didn't know?

Anna stormed back through the crowd and twisted and squeezed until she fell back out the front door.

It was a gorgeous morning. Not yet ten o'clock and the sun was bright, warming the earth outside the cabin. Anna sat down onto the little steps of the front deck, tucking her pale pink dress beneath her. She ended up painting her toes a bold, hot pink that morning before they left for church. She looked at them now, amazed at how in some ways her life had become radically different in such a short span of time. But, in others, it was much the same. At the end of the day, she was still Anna Delaney, a girl who felt like she had never really found her home in the world.

Suddenly, the crunch of gravel cut through the mid-morning air. Anna's head snapped up. Down the long drive and between the lavender bushes that peppered her parents' property drove a short convoy. In front, a beast of a blue, King cab truck with deeply tinted windows. Behind, a pearlescent SUV with three bobbing heads.

It was Dutch and his family, of course.

Anna stood, happy to reveal her excitement to the oncoming guests. She waved wildly and stepped down from the deck, brushing off the back of her dress and all of her worries from just moments before.

Dutch put his truck into park at the end of the roundabout, his father following suit. On her way to him, Anna splashed a wave through the SUV windows at sweet, little CaitlinJo, who waved a glittering doll back to her.

"Anna," Dutch breathed out as he dropped out of the truck. He wrapped her in his arms and scooped her off the earth, twirling her in a circle just as he had the night before.

"You came," she laughed into his ear.

"For you, anything," he whispered back and set her gently down again.

Anna gestured to the unloading SUV behind him.

"Does CaitlinJo know?" she asked again, and for what she hoped would be the last time. Before he could answer, CaitlinJo hopped out of the car and scrambled over, coming up under Dutch's arm.

"Happy Easter, Anna!" she squealed in delight.

"Happy Easter, CaitlinJo!" Anna replied, daintily bending down to poke the four-year-old's belly button. "What did the Easter Bunny bring you?"

"He brought me something really big," CaitlinJo's face grew wide to match her outstretched arms.

"Oh?" Anna cocked her head up at Dutch, smiling in question. "And what's that?"

"I don't know yet," CaitlinJo replied. "It's a surprise."

And with that, the little girl took off toward the garden where Anna had just been. She looked as if she always belonged there, at Anna's family cabin in Maplewood.

"CaitlinJo, wait!" Anna called after her. Her dark head turned back to reveal wide eyes. "Come here."

CaitlinJo dashed back over to Anna, who carefully pulled something out of her dress pocket. "Here, CaitlinJo. I want you to have this. Think of it as a little Easter gift."

The girl held her tiny palm out, and Anna opened her own hand, letting a delicate chain fall into the child's waiting grasp.

"A cross?" CaitlinJo looked up at Anna, pinching the silver at the end of the chain between her tiny fingers.

"CaitlinJo, my mom gave this necklace to me during an important time in my life. I've saved it in a special place ever since then. But, now I want *you* to have it."

Anna felt a tear prick at her eye as she took the chain back out of the little girl's hand, stepped behind CaitlinJo, bent, and clasped it around the girl's small neck.

CaitlinJo again held up the cross. "It's my favorite necklace ever!" she shrieked.

Anna smiled, wiping away a single tear. Wiping away a decade of tears.

CaitlinJo beamed and lunged into Anna, hugging her with all of her little might, before dashing off up to the deck to join the party that awaited her. Debbie and Bill followed, leaving Anna and Dutch together. As she passed, Debbie squeezed Anna's hand, offering her a warm, motherly smile and a quick peck on the cheek.

Anna looked back at Dutch, who also seemed to be wiping his eyes.

"I could never replace CaitlinJo's mother, Dutch. But, I'm hoping to be someone important in her life. So, maybe we can start there?"

He pulled her to a deep, brief kiss and then held her against him as they parted.

"I told CaitlinJo," he finally said.

Anna pushed back. "What?"

"I told you were a special person to us. That we might be seeing a lot more of you. I told her I love you."

Anna broke into a wide smile, her eyes bright with hope. "Well, as a matter of fact, the Easter Bunny brought *you* a surprise, too, mister," she poked Dutch in the ribs as they finally walked, Anna braced against his side, into the cabin.

"And what's that?" he asked, once they had climbed the deck and crossed the threshold. Not a moment later, they joined Debbie, Bill, and CaitlinJo as the trio opened the door and moved inside the cabin and in front of the bubbling Delaney family.

"Everyone!" Anna raised her voice over the loud celebration.

The room quieted almost instantly.

Anna flushed, nervous.

"Yes?" Bo, in her dark purple frock, prodded Anna from her station next to the kitchen table.

Anna looked at Dutch, whose eyes were on her, his eyebrows furrowed.

"Everyone, I'd like you to meet some important people." The room stayed still, expectant.

Anna barreled ahead, uncertain but determined.

"This is Debbie and Bill McCree. This beautiful girl right here is CaitlinJo," CaitlinJo waved proudly as if she were the guest of honor. Anna realized, she kind of was. The family waved back, beginning to regain their chatter. But not before Anna finally finished what she needed to say.

She licked her lips and squeezed Dutch's hand. Eyes around the room locked on her and on him. Smiles affixed. She glanced to her mom and dad, their eyebrows raised. Bo, who offered a knowing smirk. And finally back to Kurt and Mary in the far corner. Mary held up her hand in a little wave. Kurt nodded at Anna.

"Everyone, this is Dutch McCree, *my boyfriend.*"

A surprising cheer went up as the room applauded and whooped. Anna let herself laugh and took in the glory that she had long deserved.

And, for the first time in a long time, Anna Delaney felt like she had truly and finally made it home.

***

Thank you for purchasing this copy of *Return to Maplewood*. I would be honored to have your review on Amazon or Goodreads.

Elizabeth Bromke

Other Titles by Elizabeth Bromke

Christmas on Maplewood Mountain

Maplewood in Love, a Novella

Missing in Maplewood

Murder in Maplewood

Married in Maplewood

Be the first to order the next book in the series by joining my newsletter! Visit elizabethbromke.com for more information.

ACKNOWLEDGMENTS

Thank you to my growing support network of writers and advanced readers. Your early support and guidance are invaluable. The same goes for my friends, near and far.

I'd also like to spend a moment thanking my family, all of them. My own family tree has been the general inspiration for the Delaney brood. My mom, my dad, my brother, my grandmothers, grandfathers, aunts, uncles, and cousins have always been very important to me. Their continued encouragement proves that home is where the family is. What's more, the support from my extended family and in-laws is unparalleled. Were it not for the kind words and continued dedication of you all, I would not feel as proud as I do.

A special thanks to my mom, Leslie, and my husband, Ed, for staying up late and getting up early to read, reread, take notes, and offer ideas and corrections. You two are crucial to my success, and I could not move through the writing process without you. And my dear Ed, you deserve Husband of the Year for reading two sweet romance novels and taking seriously the job of writing love stories.

Finally, Eddie. You are my whole world. I write for you.

About the Author

Elizabeth Bromke is the author of the Maplewood Sisters series, a five-book saga that follows the lives of four small-town sisters, each looking for happiness. In her stories, Bromke weaves together family dynamics and the triumphs and trials of modern relationships. With the recent success of *Christmas on Maplewood Mountain (The Maplewood Sisters Prequel)*, Bromke has established herself as an emerging voice in clean, contemporary romance. Elizabeth lives down the street from her parents in the mountains of Arizona. There, she enjoys her own happily-ever-after with her husband and young son.